AF557807

THE IMMORTAL WORLD

THE IMMORTAL WORLD

SUNIL KAPOOR
SUDHIR KAPOOR

RUPA

Published by
Rupa Publications India Pvt. Ltd 2026
161-B/4, Gulmohar House,
Yusuf Sarai Community Centre,
New Delhi 110049

Sales centres
Bengaluru Chennai
Hyderabad Kolkata Mumbai

This is a work of fiction. Names, characters, places and incidents are either the product of the author's imagination or are used fictitiously and any resemblance to any actual person, living or dead, events or locales is entirely coincidental.

P-ISBN: 978-93-5352-490-6
E-ISBN: 978-93-5352-255-1

First impression 2026

10 9 8 7 6 5 4 3 2 1

Printed in India

Contents

'The soul is identical to the mind, yet different from the brain or its functions.'

'Two is not written in the usual style of a
Novel, it's a straightforward, linear narrative
Of my times, as I observed partition,
And is told through multiple characters.'

'When we understand the connection between how we live and how long we live, it's easier to make a different choice. We should see that the relationships we have are among The most powerful determinants of our well-being and survival.

PREFACE

Every story begins long before the first word is written. This one began with a feeling—quiet, persistent, and impossible to ignore. It grew in moments of observation, in unanswered questions, in the spaces between what is said and what is felt. Immortal World is the result of that accumulation.

As authors of this book titled *The Immortal World*, we have continued to follow our style of storytelling based on certain real-life incidents, blending them with fiction.

This book brings together seven stories, each different from the other. Each story explores a different idea and a different reality, but a single thread ties all of them—what remains immortal even when time, memory, belief, or life itself begins to fade.

These stories move through many worlds. If 'Immortal World' speaks of reincarnation and lives that refuse to end, 'Prison Brokers' set up in a remote part of Austria follows an artist who is trapped within his own mind, suffering from Amnesia and consequently becomes a prisoner going to the gallows for no fault of his.

The third story, 'Vazra Falls', set in the jungles of Karnataka, covers a true incident where survival in the dense jungle had become uncertain and not everyone could come out alive of the jungle infested with wild, carnivorous animals.

In 'Tulip Cobra', one explores how greed can transform some criminals into becoming serial killers in the name of what these hardened criminals believe is right.

The fifth story, once again based on a true incident in Lehran Mohabbat, a place near Bhatinda in Punjab, travels through the strength of sacrifices made by the residents of a tiny village in order to save their honour. That horrific incident actually happened in 1699 when, over a trivial issue, 682 residents of a village gave their supreme sacrifice while fighting against a massive Mughal army.

'Babloo', yet another story filled with high emotions, carries the pain of separation during the India–Pakistan partition in 1947, and is based upon a real-life incident which happened with Cricketer Sunil Gavaskar. The last one, 'Revolutionary Guru', deals with a legend surrounding a jailed convict's escape from Andaman Nicobar island and later becoming a leading Spiritual leader.

These stories are rooted in reality. What matters is not whether they are true, but what they reveal about fear, faith, memory, and human choice. This book does not offer answers. It only offers stories—meant to be felt, questioned, and carried forward.

This book is a sequel to earlier books written by the Twin Authors such as the best seller *Peacock Feather, A Ticklish Affair, A Kite in a Hurricane, The Terrible Twins, The Last Call, A Step Too Far, Punam ka Chaand, Savere ka Suraj, Save the Tiger, Hare Ram Hare Krishan, Jhoot ke Pairr Nahin, Har*

Shakh pe Ullu Baitha Hai, *Hyderabad Horror*, *The Deceitful Paramour*, *Tilanjali*, and last but not the least, ten books in the mystery solving series of *Mighty Aarav* (Twenty-five in all and ten others in the pipe line).

But for now, welcome to the world of the Immortals.

Sunil Kapoor
Sudhir Kapoor

IMMORTAL WORLD

'For if the soul exists, it is an immaterial substance and as such it is not subjected to the decomposition of material things; hence, it is immortal.'

The environment was quite calm and serene, but the path to the temple where the deities of Lava and Kusha, the sons of Lord Rama, were installed, was not so. Appukuttam and Parvati had been married for almost sixteen years but were nulliparous. They needed Mata to achieve their desire. Appukuttam held his wife's hand and said, 'Parvati, just another hundred yards or so, and the temple will be visible. Can you hear the gongs? It's nearby, please do not give up. It is a strong belief that once you receive Goddess Sita's blessings, you are blessed with a child.'

Gasping badly for breath, she asked her husband, 'Please tell me in detail as to why the old lady in the village told you to visit this temple to have a child?' Appukutam stood beside her to lend support. He replied, 'Sita denotes "soil" or "earth". It is believed that when Lord Rama abandoned Sita Devi, some seven thousand years ago, she reached Pulpally in Wayanad. She was given shelter by Sage Valmiki, who eventually wrote the epic Ramayana. Here, Luv and Kusha, the twin sons of Lord Rama, were born. It is believed that childless couples succeed in conceiving after seeking Sita Devi's blessing. Chedattin Kavu was its original name. Now it is known as the Sita Devi Lava Kusha Temple.'

In a few minutes, the tip of the brick-coloured roof of the temple became visible. They reached the temple on time to attend the *aarti* being performed by the head priest. With utmost sincerity, both of them offered prayers, and the priest blessed them with a garland and *prasad*.

The climb down from the temple, too, was difficult. They had to set their feet slowly, without getting distracted by insects and the tricky topographical conditions. Appukutam worked in the teak plantation near the Chaliyar River on a paltry wage of forty rupees a month.

After a few months, the couple were blessed with a girl child. The couple was finally content after an endless wait of seventeen years. Her birth date was 17 September 1930.

Since the child was born after they had sought the blessings of Sita Devi at Pulpally, they named the newborn 'Janaki'. As it was, Sita Devi's original name was also Janaki.

Time passed, and as Janaki turned three years old, she began speaking some words and short sentences in Malayalam, the native language of her parents. Both of Janaki's parents were illiterate, had never gone to school, but took immense pleasure in her verbosity, especially when she threw tantrums. Appukutam, along with his widowed mother, supported Janaki wholeheartedly and helped her in developing and learning to manage her own emotions. At times, because of her penchant for strange behavioural patterns such as biting, hitting, showing aggressiveness and meltdowns, they got worried. Still, they accepted that as the typical behaviour of a three-year-old.

It did seem abnormal when she screamed for a longer period of time than a normal child would. Her mother-in-law consoled Parvati by telling her regardless of whether Janaki was in the throes of the terrible twos or becoming a full-fledged three-nagger, it was a common behaviour in those parts of Wayanad.

Parvati noticed that at times Janaki would gaze at an object for a long time or keep her hands fisted, as if struggling with something that was troubling her. She would also pull her hair or throw tantrums, which were beyond their understanding. They were poor, and there was no electricity or municipal water in their village. Almost the entire village was illiterate, and superstition ran deep. It so happened that the hilly areas of Munnar and Wayanad received heavy and incessant rain during the monsoon of 1934. Parvati's only daughter was three years old and was becoming more aggressive as torrential rain swept their village. Due to heavy rains, massive landslides took place, and as a result of the landslide and terrible weather conditions, soil covered the whole three-hundred-acre plantation of coffee and tea of around the village.

The landslide was the worst of its kind in recent years. The landslide, followed by an earthquake that lasted for a few seconds, generated a tsunami in the Kabini River, with waves reaching up to ten to fifteen metres in height, bringing devastation like never before. The Kabini River, which flowed near the village, had taken a monstrous form.

Peril had surrounded the village, and it was time to take

action to control it. Appukuttam asked Parvati and his mother to leave all the belongings that they intended to carry and move to higher ground. The plateau, due to heavy rainfall and landslides, could not absorb the water, and the fluvial Kabini River was continuously rising to dangerous levels. Parvati held Janaki and moved outside the house along with her husband and mother-in-law. They realized, to their horror, that river water was gushing in on the eastern bend and would be upon them within seconds. None of the poor souls knew how to swim. Parvati quickly caught hold of the branch of a nearby tree and used her saree to tie Janaki to the upper branch of the tree. Suddenly, the rapidly moving flash floods knocked the three of them off their feet, and they were swept away in the floods, leaving their only child tied to the branch of the tree.

In the entire village, only six people had survived the natural calamity. This included Janaki, who was found tied to a branch of the tree, which had somehow withstood the onslaught of the flash flood. She had remained tied for a couple of hours and had had a harrowing time.

The aftermath of the tsunami and earthquake was unbearable as the British government left the survivors to fend for themselves. Someone from the Kalapeth village summoned the brother of Appukuttam's father, Murli, a seventy-year-old man who was living in a remote village, which was around forty kilometres from Kalapeth. He came and took custody of the hapless, traumatized Janaki, who had been rendered an orphan. Since Murli's wife had passed away and his only son was working in Hyderabad, he had only the three-year-old daughter of his nephew to care for.

Murli, at times, noticed Janaki's abnormal behaviour.

He often consulted the local *hakim* (doctor) of his village who had told him that such behaviour could be due to the psychological impact of the devastation caused by the floods, losing parents in the calamity and also being tied to a branch for several hours during the havoc wreaked by the earthquake and tsunami.

Years passed, and Janaki turned eleven. She was an obedient child and had acclimatized herself to the new environment. But off and on, she would get fits of a different kind which Murli could not comprehend. He had no idea that the intermittent explosive disorders, which resulted in Janaki's aggressive outbursts and hostility towards her neighbours without any provocation, required medical treatment.

Janaki, during such episodes, would become hostile, would shout in a different, inaudible language and explode with rage. Once, he had to summon an *ojha* (healer) who, he believed, would be able to heal her with his supernatural powers, but it resulted in no change. The healer could not cure her. She continued to have her bouts of fits, but after coming back to her senses, Janaki would be absolutely normal and would not remember anything that she had done during her outbursts. Instead of playing with other girls her age, she would often wander in the forest, totally oblivious to the dangers lurking around, the predators prowling to assuage their hunger.

Once, while looking for her in the deepest part of the forest, Murli found her playing with wolf cubs. Another time, he found her sitting close to a huge rock python, both staring at each other. Murli had to swirl his long stick to scare the python away from her. She was a loner, and that disturbed Murli quite a bit. The strange part was the fact that the eleven-year-old girl never felt threatened or fearful of the wild animals and reptiles. Once, he found her holding a large chameleon, and before he could do anything, she hit the reptile's head on a nearby rock and killed it. Her giggle thereafter scared the wits out of him.

Such behaviour could not be seen as normal. Murli could not fathom the reason for such strange behaviour. His discussion with the neighbours or the healer did not yield any results. There was no electricity, no municipal water, no school, and no facilities in the remote village where they lived.

When Janaki turned fifteen, Murli decided it was time to marry her off, and he began looking for a bridegroom for her. Rajamoli, from the nearby village, was recommended as a suitable bridegroom. The bridegroom was duly informed that Janaki at times behaved abnormally, but that that could be attributed to her traumatic experience during the floods.

Rajamoli understood and accepted his bride, whom he found to be good-looking. Murli arranged a feast with his meagre resources and performed the rituals. In three years, Janaki gave birth to a son and for the first time in her life, she felt happy and contented. Rajamoli and her son, Ram, were her true companions, and she now led an everyday life. She now had a caring husband, a chubby son and a steady income earned by Rajamoli from the job at the coffee plantation, owned by a Britisher from Manchester, Mr William Smith.

Rajamoli worked in the coffee plantations and had to reach his workplace by seven in the morning. Janaki, as a dutiful wife and mother, would look after the household chores and her nine-month-old toddler, Ram. She mingled freely with her neighbours and led an everyday life.

One day, while carrying her son in one arm and a utensil in the other, she stopped abruptly. The utensil fell, and she started screaming very badly. Although whatever she was saying was incomprehensible, her anguish was clear.

Her behaviour was hostile, and she looked at the other women accompanying her in contempt. She was angry, and her outburst was uncontrollable. Her pupils were dilated, and she continued to move her eyes from left to right, accompanied by turning of the head.

Her neighbour, Rajni, who was with her at that moment, got petrified seeing her behave like that. But within minutes, the hostilities vanished, and Janaki returned to normalcy. She did not remember anything she had said or anything about her aggressive, boorish behaviour. That day, she had shown a different side of herself to her neighbours.

In the evening, her neighbour, Rajni, came to her house and narrated the whole two minutes of the incident to Rajamoli. She told him that Janaki was blinking, squinting and rolling her eyes excessively at that point. She told him that it had scared the wits out of her. She had not witnessed such behaviour from anyone in the village till that date. She suspected that evil spirits had overtaken her for that short duration.

Rajamoli had no idea how to cure his wife. He consulted his immediate superior, who in turn spoke with the owner of the coffee plantation, Mr William Smith.

William Smith was a Britisher who was well-educated and did not believe in superstitions. According to William Smith, Rajamoli's wife had some mental disorder, and the same could be cured either by a psychiatrist or a neurologist. There were plenty of them in London who could provide help and cure Janaki through a holistic and multidisciplinary approach. But none in India would match their skill and expertise. He made arrangements for Rajamoli and Janaki to be sent to Madras Residency, where a psychiatrist was available who would try to heal Janaki scientifically.

Soon, Rajamoli and his wife travelled for the first time in a jeep provided by William Smith to Madras Residency's Christudo Hospital for medical treatment. Rajamoli had to spend considerable time convincing Janaki to undergo psychiatric treatment. She thought that undergoing such treatment was only for mad people.

But it turned out to be a unique case for the doctors who admitted her to the hospital and listened to the saga narrated by her husband. The incidents narrated were beyond the comprehension of the neurologist or psychiatrist. They were unable to decipher her disease and her occasional angry outbursts.

During her weeklong stay at the hospital, she had another attack. The doctors were taken aback as Janaki used some English words during her attack. They informed William Smith, who was also stunned by that development. 'How on earth could an illiterate woman speak English?' he wondered. The psychiatrist told him that it looked like a case of reincarnation to him. That came as a jolt to Rajamoli and Janaki.

William Smith rushed all the way to Madras Residency Hospital to understand the true nature of her mental disorder. He had held discussions on rebirth with his friend Dr Stevenson and at times had heated discussions with him on the subject.

While Dr Stevenson and William Smith were friends

and neighbours in London, Dr Stevenson had shifted from London to Canada to research cases of reincarnation; William Smith, on the other hand, had purchased a coffee plantation in Kerala and shifted to India.

William held long discussions with the psychiatrist and the other doctors and tried to reason with them about her mental state. While he was still at the hospital with the doctors, a nurse came running to them to say that Janaki had once again gone into a trance. All of them rushed to her room at the Christudo hospital to witness the incident, which turned out to be stranger than fiction.

They found Janaki in an aggressive state with her eyes rolling and both arms held upwards. She was speaking in Hindi, though some words were inaudible. Suddenly, she turned to William Smith and said in a clear tone, 'I have to die for the other one to live. I will die in exactly a month from now, on 19 September 1946.' After uttering these words, she collapsed. Everyone present there was bewildered, shocked and speechless. She had spoken in fluent English.

Here was an illiterate woman speaking in a dialect that only an educated woman would be able to utter. Moreover, how could she predict her death? What was the meaning of the other one's being able to live? Everything was baffling, and no one present could put the pieces of the jigsaw puzzle together.

On what basis could she visualize something that would happen after a month on 19 September? Everything seemed illogical to William Smith and the others present. He asked Rajamoli categorically whether Janaki had ever gone to any school. Rajamoli replied in the negative, and that intrigued the people in the room more than ever. Audible words were spoken in the English language, which Janaki was totally devoid of. Nothing more could be found out even after the sustained interrogation of Janaki. She remembered nothing.

William Smith thought of passing on the case to Dr Stevenson, who, in turn, had encountered such cases in the England Research Institute in New York, before moving to Canada to research the phenomenon of reincarnation. Dr Stevenson had researched the Pollock sisters and other cases of reincarnation and was an authority on the subject.

On receiving a letter from William Smith, Stevenson immediately left for India and reached just in time to witness the drama which unfolded on 19 September 1946 at Rajamoli's house in Kelapeth in Wayanad, Kerala.

The entire village had, by then, come to know about the prophecy of Janaki about her own death. Some people thought that she was under the influence of some evil spirits. William Smith and Dr Stevenson tried to disperse the crowd that was beginning to gather outside the small house of Rajamoli. The villagers wanted to witness whether the prophecy would be fulfilled.

Nothing happened from morning to late afternoon of 19 September. It started to drizzle, and some villagers returned to their respective homes. Rajamoli loved Janaki. He did not allow her to cook food or go to the river to fetch water. He did not even allow her to touch their son. The son was to be looked after by their neighbour Rajni that day.

The drizzle turned into a downpour, and nearly all the villagers left the vicinity. A bout of fit struck Janaki, but this time she did not become aggressive. She started shivering, and it seemed as if she was trying to fight with herself. As if someone wanted to leave her body, and she was trying to stop the soul or spirit from doing so. Her eyes rolled, and she eventually collapsed.

She was soon declared dead by the doctor who was in attendance. Dr Stevenson had brought a camera with him, and he was able to capture the entire incident on it. On hearing about her death, the villagers come over to Rajamoli's house and suggested that he perform her last rites as quickly as possible. She had some evil spirit in her, and they wanted to burn the body as soon as possible.

However, due to heavy rains, no arrangements for dry wood could be made to burn her lifeless body. The doctor wanted to perform an autopsy on the body, but Rajamoli turned down the request and insisted on being allowed to perform the last rites.

It took them around an hour to make all the arrangements and perform the last rites, as per the prevalent customs. Janaki's body was lying on the funeral pyre as Rajamoli, sobbing, lit the fire. Suddenly, Janaki stirred and sat up.

It was a miracle of some sort. Villagers who had gathered at the funeral pyre ran away shouting, 'Ghost! Ghost!' They kept yelling, 'She is evil, and evil shall befall the village. She must die; she must die!'

Dr Stevenson and William Smith, who were about to leave for their respective destinations from the guest house, were recalled because of the strange happening. They rushed back to the open field, where Janaki, who had been lying on the funeral pyre stone dead, had regained consciousness.

Janaki was dressed in a red-coloured saree. This was the

custom followed by the villagers. Dr Stevenson reached the spot and spoke to Janaki but received no response. Getting up, she started speaking in a mixture of Hindi and English. Everyone present was fully aware that Janaki spoke Malayalam, knew no English, and knew a little Hindi. She spoke aloud, 'Why do you keep calling me Janaki? I am Jagrani. I belong to Kanpur.' She then looked at Dr Stevenson and said in fluent English, 'Sir, what am I doing here in this place. Who are all of you? Why is this man trying to touch me?' Dr Stevenson replied, 'Janaki or Jagrani, whoever you may be, the man who is trying to touch you is your husband. You have a one-year-old son. You are not Jagrani of Kanpur but Janaki of Kelapeth in Wayanad, Kerala.'

'No, sir,' pat came her reply. 'Why should I lie to you. sir, you seem to be a good person. Please tell me how I ended up here in Kerala. I am a resident of Arya Nagar, Kanpur. I have married Professor Jagannath, living at 58/3 Vishnupuri. He is a lecturer at Kanpur University. I have two sons, Devendernath and Surendernath. What has happened to them? Where am I, and why am I here, sir?' she asked, baffled.

Dr Stevenson said, 'I think you should rest for a while and then we shall talk. Your brain and heart may not be able to take so much stress and strain.'

'No, sir, I am perfectly all right,' she replied, looking straight at the doctor. I want to go to Kanpur and be with my husband and my family. Suddenly, her head started aching, and she lost consciousness.

But for Dr Stevenson, everybody else was shell-shocked upon hearing what Janaki, alias Jagrani, had uttered. Tears rolled down Rajamoli's face. He was very much in love with his wife, who had been his companion for some time and had brought a tremendous change in his life. He was holding his son; a wonderful gift she had given him. But now the same person was behaving oddly. She was refusing to accept that she was Janaki and had been speaking fluently in English, which even he could not understand.

Dr Stevenson waited for the reincarnated soul of Jagrani, who was now very much incarnated in Janaki, to regain consciousness. Once she was conscious, he asked her in English, 'Who are you, and why do you say you belong to Kanpur. Do you not recognize your son and husband, who are very much present here?'

She looked at the two he had pointed his fingers at and said, 'Sorry, sir, I do not know them.' She spoke English fluently, without mincing her words. She also emphasized the words 'do not'. She spoke again to Dr Stevenson, 'Believe me, Sir, I am Jagrani, or affectionately, Rani, of Vishnupuri, Kanpur. I do not know why I am here. It seems that I have woken from a deep slumber and am astonished that I have reached Kerala. I know Kerala is a part of India and is located in the southwestern part, but I belong to Kanpur, *Kanpur*, sir.'

She paused for some time and then continued, 'My brothers work in Elgin Mills, which manufactures cloth and towels. I am a graduate of Kanpur University. I am married to Professor Jagannath. My father is a schoolteacher, and he encouraged all three of his daughters to study and become graduates. In fact, we are the only family in the entire Arya Nagar area that had not one but three graduates.' She continued to speak about her past life without realizing the fact that in this life, she had been born in Kerala as Janaki.

But then, Rani was shown a mirror, and this time it was her time to be shell-shocked. She shrieked the moment she saw her image in the mirror. 'What has happened to my face, my hair, my fair complexion? I was born as Rani Tandon and became Jagrani Mehrotra after marrying Professor Jagannath. What am I doing here? Oh my god! Oh! My god! Now I remember I was...' she stopped and then started crying and said 'killed'. She again lost consciousness.

Dr Stevenson withdrew and went out and told her husband, 'Sorry, Raja, extremely sorry, but she is the reincarnation of Rani of Kanpur. She is under tremendous stress; she might go mad and turn into an aggressive lunatic. We shall leave her for now and come back later when she is relaxed and in her senses. She must be allowed complete bed rest to cope with having two personalities embedded in her mind. Please do not ask me how this happens. What is the logic behind this, or what is the basis or genesis of this phenomenon? No one knows.' He concluded in one breath, to the astonishment and bewilderment of Rajamoli. Rajamoli had no room for any misgivings; only tears kept rolling down his face. His normal life had suddenly taken a dramatic turn. The spirit or soul of two separate women now existed in his wife.

Janaki woke up after being unconscious for over fourteen hours. She did not speak a word. She searched for a piece of paper and wrote a letter to Jagannath of Kanpur and asked Rajamoli to post it. Rajamoli complied, and as forewarned by Dr Stevenson, he did not ask any questions but offered her Malayali food cooked in the traditional way. She refused to eat it. She was not accustomed to having Malayali food. His neighbour came to his rescue by bringing north Indian food consisting of kidney beans baked in tart tomatoes, spices, ginger and garlic. She ate that food with rice wholeheartedly, and a smile came to her lips.

Dr Stevenson visited Rajamoli to find him, along with Janaki, participating in the 'Rath Yatra' taking place in the nearby town. An almost one-kilometre-long procession of boys, some dressed as Lord Krishna, was underway. Although Janaki did come to the town to witness the long procession moving towards a Hindu temple some three kilometres away and remained with Rajamoli, she was a mute spectator to the festivities.

Dr Stevenson continued to observe her lack of interest in the procession. She now also liked North Indian food and was averse to having South Indian delicacies. He inferred that Janaki's spirit had moved away, and that the body now had the soul or spirit of Jagrani alias Rani.

A month passed, when Ram Kishan, the younger brother of Jagannath, entered the small village and enquired about Jagrani. He was immediately taken to Dr Stevenson, who met him and narrated the entire incident of Janaki's conversion to Jagrani. He told Ram Kishan that after she claimed she was Rani and not Janaki, she had mostly remained silent and spent her time wandering through the forest or sitting on the banks of the Kabini River.

To his surprise, Ram Kishan confirmed the entire narrative of Rani. However, he differed from Rani on the issue of her death. While Rani had mentioned that she had been killed, Ram Kishan maintained that she had met with an accident. While cooking food, her saree had caught fire, and she had succumbed to her burns. He confirmed that Rani had died in 1930, around the time when Janaki was born and he also informed Dr Stevenson of Jagannath's demise some two years earlier.

Dr Stevenson took him to Rani but asked him not to speak as he intended not to disclose his identity to her. Rani was sitting outside her house with her one-year-old son, whom she had accepted, albeit reluctantly.

Dr Stevenson, while approaching her, said, 'Look Rani, here is your husband, Jagannath. He has come all the way from Kanpur on receiving your letter.' Rani raised her eyebrows, smiled and said, 'He is not my husband. He is Ram Kishan, my brother-in-law. He looks much older living in the same house.' Ram Kishan touched her feet, though he was almost twenty years older than the woman sitting in front of her. Rani spoke again, 'Ram *bhai*, where is Rukmani these days. Did she marry that scoundrel, Guddan, the hooligan of Chunni Ganj?' He looked quizzically at Dr Stevenson and Rajamoli. Dr Stevenson understood and, with a puzzled expression, said, 'Mr Kishan, I am doing a tremendous amount of research in the field of reincarnation, and believe me, in London, New York, Canada, some children have made strange claims of reincarnation, but on growing older, they have forgotten about it. However, in this case, strangely enough, Janaki has given minute details about the life of Rani; every detail given by her matches with that of Rani's life, which seems to have been cut short by someone who despised her.'

Ram Kishan again gave a bewildered look. A strange woman who did not resemble his dead sister-in-law was taking their names as if she knew them well. One by one, he showed her the photographs that he had brought. She recognized all the relations, friends, and also her husband who was there in those photographs. She stopped and glared at one photograph for a long time and then said, 'Ram bhai, you have not answered my question. Where is she? I want to meet her. I have a score to settle with her.' Ram Kishan looked at Dr Stevenson and asked him in Hindi, 'Sir, what is she talking about? How on Earth can this be possible? I have never witnessed such a thing in my life. Next, I will find a boy talking about having being reborn as Jagannath. I do not understand what is happening here.'

'Exactly,' replied Dr Stevenson, 'that's what I have been saying. But the spirit is not evil. Spirit or soul, whatever you may call it Mr Ram Kishan. Lord Krishan, in his sermons, has always maintained that one can kill the material body, the one that has lived up to his or her time, but cannot kill the soul. The soul is immortal and drifts into the immortal world and is reincarnated in another body.'

He continued, 'There are many cases of rebirth. Take, for example, the case of Andrea Leininger's two-year-old son James, who was believed to have died in a plane crash and was in fact James Houstan of Pennsylvania, USA.'

About fourteen to fifteen years back, Shanti Devi of Delhi claimed to be the reincarnation of Lugdi Devi born in Mathura. She had provided many specific details about Lugdi Devi and even told her parents and me that she had died eleven years back while giving birth to a child.

Ram Kishan understood the reason for the strange behaviour of Janaki, who was the reincarnation of Jagrani. Jagrani kept repeating the sentence, 'I want to meet her; I want to meet her. I have to settle with her; I seek revenge.'

Then she became unconscious once again. Ram Kishan once again questioned Dr Stevenson, 'Sir, this is Kerala, Jagrani was in Kanpur, how is this possible? Do you mean the soul has travelled all the way to Kerala? Isn't it absurd? It is so strange and difficult to fathom Rani's soul taking the body of an infant Janaki sometime in 1930. This is 1946, sir. Jagrani died more than twelve years ago, and now her two sons are older than the woman in front of me.'

Dr Stevenson replied with a smile, 'Mr Kishan, there is the case of Ram Behain from Bihar who claimed that he was Sohan Singh of Ludhiana, Punjab. He did so until the age of five, and later, when he grew into adulthood, he forgot all about his past life.'

Rajamoli, Dr Stevenson and Ram Kishan decided to take her to Kanpur and test her memories. The next day, they bought train tickets, and after an arduous two-day travel, they would reach Kanpur.

But before reaching Kanpur, the train stopped at Unnao, Uttar Pradesh. Dr Stevenson enquired about whether they had reached Kanpur Junction from Ram Kishan, and before he could reply, Jagrani said, 'No sir, this is Unnao, which comes before Kanpur. Another twenty minutes or so and we should reach Kanpur Junction, the last station was Nawabganj, which is about fifty kilometres from Kanpur.' Rajamoli asked her in his slackened Hindi, 'How do you know about Nawabganj and Unnao?' She instantly replied, 'I was born in Nawabganj. My father, who was a teacher, got a job in Kanpur much later.'

Kanpur Junction came, and she recognized it. Jagrani, duly charged up with emotions, said, 'There is a clock tower outside the station. My husband used to match the time on his watch with the clock on the tower.'

She reached the outskirts of the railway station and said in disbelief, 'Nothing has changed, same clock tower, same rickshaw stand and same eateries. My god! Nothing seems to have changed in the last twenty years. Only I was not here...'

Dr Stevenson stated, 'Jagrani, can you recollect where you were after you were killed?' 'No, sir,' she replied rather emphatically, 'but I certainly plan to punish the evil doers.' Dr Stevenson probed further, 'Who was he? Or was it a female?'

Rani looked at Dr Stevenson and said, 'Who else but my sister-in-law and that ruffian paramour of hers! The scoundrel poured kerosene on me and lit a fire with his own matchstick. Within seconds, I was a burning inferno, and then it was nothing but oblivion.'

Raising his eyebrows, Rajamoli enquired, 'How on Earth are you going to nail them? Who will believe you, dear?' Rani gave him an angry look and retorted, 'Please do not call me "dear". I am not your wife. I was married to the pious, humble person known as Professor Jagannath. He had no idea what his younger sister was up to, and what she would end up doing to me.'

Ram Kishan stopped walking along with them and halted midway. All of them were walking towards the rickshaw stand and were surprised at his reaction. He slowly uttered, 'Jagannath is no more. He died last year from a lung infection. The doctors called it acute pneumonia.'

Rani had been hoping to meet her husband. This news disturbed her, but she somehow controlled her grief. All of them walked silently towards the rickshaw which took them towards Vishnupuri Colony. Rani gave directions to the rickshaw puller, and they soon reached the temple near the late Jagannath's house. Rani refused to enter the house and meet her two grown-up sons, who were older than her in age.

On the contrary, she told Ram Kishan, her brother-in-law in her past life, to keep this sensational news a secret till she was able to expose Guddan, the Hooligan, and Rukmani. She left for a guest house on the mall Road, along with Rajamoli and Dr Stevenson.

In the evening, Dr Stevenson visited his old, trusted friend, who had been transferred from Hyderabad to Kanpur as Superintendent of Police. On listening to the story narrated by Dr Stevenson about Jagrani's spirit being in the mortal body of Janaki, he found it to be a unique case which was also a tad difficult to believe. At first, the Superintendent did not believe a word of it. But later, after meeting Jagrani and questioning her for an hour, he understood the reality of the Immortal World.

The Superintendent, after listening to the entire story, struck his palm on the desk and said, 'I know how to make them admit their crime! This weekend, there is a play being staged at the auditorium at the police lines. We can invite the two of them to the show. We will compile the script with Jagrani's help and replicate on stage exactly what happened some twenty years ago on the day she was killed. That might do the trick, and they might confess to their crime.'

The time was too short, but Jagrani explained to the scriptwriter in detail the manner in which she was killed by the two. The scriptwriter was told to maintain secrecy. He, too, was mesmerized and intrigued by the true incident narrated by Jagrani.

Two different people approached the hooligan, Guddan, and his ex-paramour, Rukmani. Guddan had no qualms in coming over to the police lines to witness the show, as he had become an informer of the police. He had been caught while smuggling contraband liquor, and to save his skin, he had first turned approver and, later, a loyal informer. He had also started to help the newly elected minister of coal and mines organize rallies and mobilize people for him.

Rukmani had to be cajoled by one of her close friends into attending the play. On the assigned weekend, the duo arrived, and the arrangements were made in such a way that Jagrani, Dr Stevenson, Guddan and Rukmani sat in the same row. Rukmani had no idea as to why the lady sitting next to her kept on staring at her. She was already uncomfortable sitting with her ex-boyfriend, but a South Indian lady continuously staring at her was beyond annoying.

The show started with a man and a woman engaging in intimacy. Another woman walked in and, on seeing the two, shouted at them, 'So, that's what happens when I am not home.' The girl who was acting as the sister-in-law, shrieked and said, 'See, I told you, she can come anytime, and you were stupid enough not to listen to me.' The paramour got up and, while pointing a finger at the intruder, said, 'You will not tell anybody about this. Soon, I am going to get married to the daughter of a wealthy industrialist. If you tell people, then my marriage might get cancelled.' The actor playing Jagrani replied, 'No way, I am going to shout and call people here. I am going to tell the entirety of Kanpur that despite being engaged to someone, you are having an affair with my sister-in-law.'

In the play, Jagrani moved towards the door, but the

paramours swiftly reached the exit before her and forcibly stopped her from going out of the house. A scuffle breaks out, and the paramour hits her with a table fan, lying nearby. Jagrani starts to bleed, but she rushes out to the verandah. Both of them try to stop her from going out on the street. The paramour hits her again. This time, he uses a brick lying nearby, and Jagrani falls. She gets up and kicks the paramour in the stomach and tries to rush to the main exit door. However, the paramour pulls her back, and encircles a shawl around Jagrani's neck. Rukmani also comes to his help, and in the spur of the moment, both of them strangle Jagrani, who gasps for breath, and then succumbs and falls to the ground.

The paramour rushes to the kitchen and pours kerosene all over the dead body and lights it with a matchstick. All this was being portrayed just as it had happened to Jagrani twelve years back. Meanwhile, the Superintendent continued to observe the couple who were looking extremely nervous. Rukmani realized that there was something wrong and could not take it anymore. She rushed out of the auditorium and looked like she had lost her nerve.

The Superintendent rushed out after her. The Sub-Inspector had already been posted at the exit door of the auditorium. He was holding an old photograph of Jagrani given by Ram Kishan. She was arrested along with the ex-paramour, Guddan, and taken to the police station. She was so petrified that she fainted.

When she regained consciousness, she found herself in the police station with her ex-boyfriend. Around fifteen armed policemen were staring at them. Superintendent Ved Prakash broke the silence and said, 'Your game is up, Rukmani. We have a witness who has narrated the entire incident of you and Guddan killing Jagrani some twelve years back. You will go to jail for at least fourteen years, or you might be hanged till death.'

Rukmani started howling and said, 'It was not me, sir. He hit her first with an iron fan and later with a brick. He was the one who doused her with kerosene oil and set Jagrani on fire.'

Then, Janaki—alias Jagrani—walked in, 'Do you recognize me, Rukmani? Weren't you the one who came and whispered in Jagrani's ears that she was looking stunning? Weren't you the one who took fifty rupees from your elder brother before leaving the room on Jagrani's wedding night?' Rukmani looked aghast and did not say a word, and her facial expression turned pale.

Guddan said a little vehemently, 'I know some politician, and I want to meet them. I am being charged for an offence which I never committed. I was never responsible for the death of Jagrani.'

The Superintendent of Police asked Guddan, 'Sure, but please answer my three questions. First, why is it that it is only the daughters-in-law whose clothes catch fire while cooking and not any other family members? Can you give me one instance where a sister-in-law or mother-in-law has received a burn injury that has resulted in their death? Not even once has it ever come to light that a sister-in-law has died from burn injuries. Only daughters-in-law die of burns in our country. Secondly, if it was an accident and you were present on the spot, then why didn't you call for an ambulance or a doctor? And thirdly, why did both of you abstain from helping the victim douse the fire? If you can answer these three questions, you can go scot-free; otherwise, you will face trial, and I will personally see to it that Jagrani gets justice.'

Rukmani intervened, 'H-he is the one who set Jagrani on fire. He is the one who killed her, and who is this dark woman? How does she know about what I said to Jagrani on her wedding night?'

The police recorded her statement and arrested both of them on charges of killing Jagrani. She had gotten her revenge. She went to her house for the first time after coming to Kanpur all the way from Wayanad. She met her two sons, and it took them a while to digest the presence of the stranger and her fictional story, which was explained to them by Ram Kishan. He uttered in the end, 'She is your mother Jagrani, though in the body of Janaki. She belongs to the Immortal World.'

Of late, she had been having some concussion in her brain, as if Janaki were struggling with Jagrani to establish her identity. It looked as if, having exacted her revenge, Jagrani also wanted to exit the body of Janaki and leave Janaki to live her life.

A few days later, Jagrani's sons started witnessing her having concussions and falling at times, too. They called Dr Stevenson and asked him to come and check up on her.

Within a few days, as Dr Stevenson came back to check up on Janaki to complete his theory, Janaki started behaving abruptly, and as Dr Stevenson was recording all of it on his camera, Janaki started rolling her eyes, and within no time, she collapsed.

After an hour of waiting, as Dr Stevenson was about to declare her dead, Janaki woke up. Dr Stevenson asked, 'How are you feeling now, Jagrani?' But this time, Janaki gave no reply. She started speaking Malayalam, and Dr Stevenson understood that it was no longer Jagrani but Janaki's soul itself in Janaki's body.

2024 brought misfortune to many more families in Wayanad, including Janaki's. Every year, 175 million children globally are affected by such natural disasters. New cases of relatives contacting the organization looking to reunite with loved ones have increased by almost ninety per cent over time. Just like Janaki, many nerves were frayed. Many hearts were broken forever from the floods that remade the Earth, from the flood that changed two lives for the better.

PRISON BROKERS

The capital was reeling in the grip of summer, with an intense heatwave wrapping the city in a suffocating embrace. The flight to Vienna, Austria, was due to depart at 3 p.m. from Indira Gandhi International Airport, New Delhi, but was delayed due to a technical snag. Sabina was tired of waiting for the flight to depart. The combination of being alone and the feeling of uncertainty made the wait seem endless. What was amusing her was the chatter and curious glances from the bunch of youngsters sitting across from her. Sabina Ramani was used to such attention, and at times she frowned at the lewd remarks, which were aimed at her. She was tall, fair and attractive, which gave her the confidence to handle any situation. She was a budding lawyer en route to Austria for an exchange programme, initiated by the Bar Council of India.

At around 9 p.m., an announcement was made that Air India Flight AI 115 was ready to depart for Vienna. The delay had added to Sabina's woes, as she was to take a connecting flight from Vienna to Klagenfurt, which was around 300 kilometres from her destination, Villach—a city in southern Austria. There was a chance she would miss her flight to Klagenfurt, and the irony was that she could not blame anyone for her plight. The staff and crew members were brusque and unapologetic. She had no option but to travel since it was the only direct flight to Vienna from New Delhi. While Klagenfurt was a busy city with traffic and business, Villach was a quiet town. As a matter of fact, it was only a tiny village at the time. Still, it came into prominence after a Munich-based giant of a company, Infineon Inc., decided to set up its manufacturing unit there. The company manufactured semiconductors. Sabina was looking forward to spending some good time in an advanced country and gaining valuable experience in legal matters.

After a hectic and eventful eight hours, she finally reached Vienna. The delay was further compounded by the fact that the plane had to take a different route altogether. When she questioned the steward about it, she was told that the detour was necessary due to a ban imposed by Pakistan.

Sabina had undertaken training with a reputed law firm in Connaught Place, New Delhi. The law firm did all the legal work for its counterparts in Austria. She had applied for an exchange training program with her counterparts in Austria, and in turn, an Austrian was supposed to join the Indian firm to learn about the laws prevailing in India.

It was close to midnight when the plane landed at Vienna airport. Sabina was stranded at Vienna Airport. She approached the information desk for help, but there was no other flight before the next morning.

Sabina could not decide whether to wait at the lounge or to check herself into a nearby hotel. Before she could decide, an Indian, in an inebriated condition, approached her. He too was seeking some information from the information desk, and, noticing Sabina, a good-looking girl, he seized the opportunity to 'help' the 'damsel in distress'. He tried to convince her that if she had any trouble finding a good hotel, she could stay with him at his place, as he was a resident of Vienna and knew the city like the back of his hand. He was foolish enough to state that after spending a night with him, she could catch a flight or a train to Klagenfurt as was convenient to her. He may have been a genuine person concerned about a compatriot in a foreign country, but Sabina had no desire to go anywhere with him. Sensing Sabina's reluctance, he asked her if he could drop her at a nearby guesthouse that offered accommodation and could be considered an absolutely safe place to spend the night.

Sabina, however, preferred to remain at the airport and spend the night there. But he was persistent, and without showing much decency, he grabbed her arm. Sabina screamed for help, and the scene suddenly morphed into a ruckus. The security staff at the airport came running to her rescue and firmly told the drunkard to leave the lady alone before they arrested him on charges of molestation and inappropriate conduct. The drunkard immediately let go of her arm, sobered down, apologized and hurried towards the Ausgang.

Almost everybody at the airport spoke German, and most of the signboards were in the same language. Sabina, with great difficulty, lay down on a sofa with her luggage next to her. She was petrified. This was the very first time she was travelling alone, and it was turning out to be a nightmare. Sabina had a diner's card that gave her access to the lounge, and she preferred to spend the night there only.

It was nearly 2 a.m. Sabina felt nervous when she realized that she was all alone in that huge lounge. When she had landed in Vienna a few hours ago, there had been a lot of hustle and bustle. But now there was an eerie silence. She calmed down a little when she noticed one person, who looked like an Asian, mopping the floor at a distance. Scared but determined, Sabina waited for dawn. Just then she heard an announcement stating that Flight AI 115, which had landed two hours ago from Delhi, was now ready to depart back to Delhi. Alarmed, she rushed to the baggage carousel and searched anxiously for her luggage, but her suitcases were nowhere to be found.

Recently, there had been many incidents of airport staff breaking open suitcases and stealing cash and valuables. She had heard about such incidents and that was the reason why she had hidden the Euros in the box of sweets but someone from the staff working at the lounge had stolen the hidden Euros, too. In disgust, she sat on the couch. 'I left my luggage here for fifteen minutes, and it was intact, while the workers at Delhi's airport had the time to open my suitcase, search for the money hidden there, and steal it! God! I feel like killing them with my bare hands. I will never travel by that airline ever,' she vowed. She was angry. 'What a beginning! First, the flight got delayed due to a technical snag. Second, I missed my flight to Klagenfurt. Then, a brush-up with a drunkard, and now, I have lost what Satish Uncle gave me. Ok Sabina, keep it up. You will go far.' She threw her hands upwards in exasperation and squirmed once again.

Her anger simmered down when she thought about her mother, who had to struggle throughout her life to maintain the house and her two fatherless children. She exclaimed, 'Oh, what I am facing now is nothing compared to what she has faced all these years.' Exhausted to the hilt, she dozed off.

Sabina Ramani was a fatherless child. Her father, Gulshan Ramani, had been an artist, a sculptor par excellence. But art was neither promoted in India in the eighties nor was it saleable. When Sabina was born, her father was thirty-four years old and was making ends meet by painting film posters. He could sometimes sell his paintings and sculptures, but only with difficulty. When she was two years old, her father, aged thirty-six, had had a brain stroke. The operation cost seven lakh rupees, which could not be raised even after all her mother's jewellery had been sold. Satish, her maternal uncle, had come to their rescue and supported them in their hour of need. Sabina's mother, Rashmi, was his only sister. He helped them against his wife's wishes who berated him for being overly magnanimous. 'Rashmi married the poverty-stricken artist without your approval. She ran away with the so-called good-for-nothing artist. Let them rot and handle their affairs,' she would often tell her husband. She would fight with Satish over Sabina's parents, telling him he was being a sentimental fool. 'Sister or no sister, money is more important than any relationship,' she would scoff at her husband.

After the operation was performed by Dr Sanjiv Malik, it became clear that her father had developed other deficiencies because of the stroke. One of them was acute dementia. He, at times, appeared to be unaware of his existence. After coming home from the hospital, he would, sometimes look at his wife blankly and remember absolutely nothing. On other occasions, coming back from a friend's place, he would suddenly forget the way to his house and sit on a bench affixed on a pavement in a park for hours, till his wife, frantically searching for him, found him and brought him back to the house. It was a scary affair, and Rashmi Ramani often had to take leave from school to be with her husband, so that he would not stray too far from the house or get into trouble.

Once, when his wife, five-year-old daughter and three-year-old son were at school, he had gone to attend the funeral of one of his close friends. While his friend's body was at the funeral pyre, something shifted in his mind. He completely lost his sense of direction and could not find his way back to the flat. He somehow reached the railway station, boarded the train without knowing its destination and never returned home. Frantic calls were made to relatives and friends. Rashmi struggled to bring up two children all by herself. Satish Uncle lodged an FIR and placed advertisements in the newspapers, but to no avail. The search for her father led nowhere, even though the police investigated the disappearance of Gulshan Ramani for several weeks.

Rashmi's husband, Gulshan, wasn't an artist of his age and had neither the luck nor the talent of other senior artists like Amar Nath Sehgal or Maqbool Fida Husain. On the contrary, Rashmi had to cope with the strange behavioural changes of her husband. Initially, Rashmi had assumed that her husband was frustrated for not being able to adequately provide for them, but later she began to sense that something deeper was amiss. Gulshan would sit for hours staring at the wall or give her a blank look when she asked him a simple question. Rashmi's pent-up loneliness and frustration erupted in several skirmishes between husband and wife. Gulshan would get aggressive about a trivial issue, and then it would be difficult to quieten him.

When Gulshan vanished for good, Rashmi had no money and no assets to fall back on except the two-bedroom flat. She continued her teaching job at the nearby school and had her five-year-old daughter enrolled there as well. However, it's another matter that she often felt Sabina missed her father, especially at birthday parties when she saw her friends being affectionately pampered by their fathers. Rashmi tried to explain to Sabina that everyone in the world had their share of sufferings. Some had lost their parents, others were struggling with chronic disease or acute financial problems, but to all this Sabina would retort with, 'But mother, we seem to have all of the problems. Neither is my father here nor do we have money. I wear old and torn clothes. My friends laugh at me. Last time you bought me a new dress and I wore it to a birthday party, my friends laughed and asked if I had borrowed it from someone.'

Rashmi had a tough time bringing up her two fatherless children. Her close friend, Mrs Shukla Sehgal, wife of M. Amarnath Sehgal, the famous painter, often gave them financial support and also got her children enrolled in the famous Modern School at Barakhamba Road, New Delhi. This brought some relief to the two children of Rashmi Ramani as they indeed enjoyed their tenure in Modern School where values were painstakingly inculcated and imbibed in the students.

Sabina was startled out of her slumber by a sudden announcement at the airport. How had she slept through all the noise? She quickly went to the washroom and then boarded the 8:15 a.m. flight to Klagenfurt, one of Austria's bustling cities. The scenery from the window was breathtaking, she saw beautiful lakes and the snow-covered peaks of the Alps shimmering below her. She had seen the film *Sound of Music*, which had been shot entirely in Austria. But this was for real. She had been told by her friend that the National anthem of Austria had a mention of '*Land der berge, land a strome*', meaning, 'Land of the mountains, Land by the river'. It was the first time that she was witnessing it in person. Austria was indeed beautiful, to say the least.

The plane landed at Klagenfurt Airport in forty minutes, and within another ten minutes, she was out of the airport. She inquired about taxi hire charges and was told that it would cost around seventy euros to Villach. She shelved the idea of taking a taxi and decided to travel by an ÖBB train, which would cost her only fifteen euros to reach her destination. After all, she was left with only a hundred euros courtesy of the wretched thieves at the Delhi International Airport.

After taking directions, she started walking towards the station but got confused because all the signs were in German, a language she did not understand. She had no idea that 'Ausgang' meant exit and 'Hauptbahnhof' meant a central station. Noticing her confusion, Nikhil, a young Indian compatriot and an engineer by profession, walked towards her to help. He was congenial and etiquette personified, as any gentleman would be, and fortunately for her, had come to see one of his friends off at the Klagenfurt Airport.

'Excuse me, miss! Are you an Indian?' She nodded. 'I am Nikhil. Can I be of any help to you?' he asked politely, bowing down a little. 'Yes, please. How can I reach the central station? I have to go to Villach.'

'Well, firstly, it's pronounced "Fillach". The station here is known as Hauptbahnhof. Don't worry, when you start living here, you'll quickly figure out the language. It's easy. The "V" is pronounced as "F", Volkswagen is pronounced Foxwagen and the name of the city Veldon is pronounced as "Feldon",' he said, showing off his grasp of the German language and his knowledge of the places in Austria a tad. 'And Madame, I reiterate that Villach is pronounced as Fillach; that's what you should state while buying a ticket at the counter.'

She grimaced and could only utter thanks quite feebly. He walked her to Hauptbahnhof, which was nearby, and was courteous enough to procure a ticket for her despite her protests. She thanked Nikhil profusely and bid him goodbye. Within minutes, she was en route to Villach on one of the ÖBB trains running through Austria. At last, she breathed a sigh of relief and settled down. She had exchanged phone numbers with Nikhil and now she sent him a message thanking him for his help. He had been courteous enough to walk her up to the ÖBB train, reducing her anxiety to a great extent. 'All's well that ends well,' she grimaced while enjoying the pure scenic beauty of nature. Soon the ÖBB reached Villach. She got down at the station, walked to the nearby Holiday Inn, and checked in.

The next day, Sabina reported to her immediate superior, Maria Schneider, the senior partner in the law firm. She had to undergo a month of training before handling the legal work that was to be assigned to her. The office, located on the first floor above Bernold Restaurant, overlooked the Drava River, which flowed through the cities of Sheldon and Wörthersee. From the window, she could observe the movement of traffic and could see Austrians on the adjoining bridge and Haus Platz—the only major market square of Villach.

The area where the employers had put her up was disappointing. It was almost unliveable. She had been allotted a room in an old house in a congested area. It had seen better days. Its flourish of frescoes, alcoves and archways were all gone. Instead, it had a dimly lit gallery, a small porch and one claustrophobic room which she would have to share with Rita, another Indian employed by the law firm. Sabina was unhappy with the accommodation, but could do nothing about it. That irked her more.

Well, what else could she have expected? Villach had long been a village whose fortunes had changed when a multinational company, Infineon Inc., brought significant development to the town. Another company, Bernard Infrastructure Inc., provided the necessary logistical support to the six hundred employees of Infineon Inc., but she would have to make do with whatever her employers had provided. After all, at the beginning of her career, she could not ask for more. Her uncle had once said, 'Sabina, learning to ignore certain things is one of the greatest paths to inner peace.'

Sabina was quick enough to learn the nuances of legal work in the law firm. Their main clients in Villach were Infineon Inc., Bernard Infrastructure Inc., Casino Veldon, Hotel Holiday Inn, and the newly opened Hotel Seven. She worked relentlessly and soon became part of the team that handled the legal drafting of contracts for clients. The senior lawyer Maria Schneider was not only flexible but also motivated Sabina by telling her that successful people didn't relax. They, in fact, relax by doing some work.

Nikhil and Sabina also began to develop a relationship; on the other hand, she was in constant touch with her mother on the phone and had been candid enough to tell her that, besides working hard in the firm, she was also dating Nikhil Chopra. He seemed like a nice guy. Nikhil Chopra was a typical Punjabi from Amritsar: tall, good-looking, and chivalrous to the core. He was a confident person. Having spent a couple of years in Austria, he knew a great deal about the cities and what there was to see.

Once, Sabina went out with Nikhil on a date to Sheldon, where they played at the slot machines at Jared Casino. Later, they were at McDonald's waiting in a queue. Two boys in front of them were so engrossed in their discussions that they failed to notice that people in the queue had moved ahead. Sabina asked Nikhil to push them just a little, but he did not move and, in a hushed tone, asked her to be patient.

Later, while sitting down to have their burgers, Nikhil confessed about a bad experience he had had a few months back. While standing in a similar queue, he had pushed a seven-year-old child and unintentionally touched his buttocks. The child had complained to his mother, who, in turn, had summoned the police. Nikhil was arrested for an act of obscenity. Sabina, outraged, said, 'What's so obscene about it? When some stubborn, ill-mannered child or youngster is blocking the queue, you have to push him a little! I don't see anything wrong with it.'

'No, Sabina, not in Austria or any part of Europe or even in the US. It is an offence to touch a child inappropriately. I was put behind bars, and charges were framed against me. My immediate boss understood that I was innocent and had put his legal team behind me. With great difficulty, I was bailed out after one week upon my pleading guilty and paying a fine of two thousand euros. The courts are very strict and firm on such issues, whether you are at fault or not. If you are in Rome, live the way the Romans do.' He smiled and continued his saga.

'I was devastated, but that is what one must learn while being in a foreign land. You are a lawyer. You would certainly know the laws of this land. But I am an engineer. How on Earth could I have known about this law?' Both of them laughed over the incident and continued with their meal.

Six months passed in a flash, and Sabina became the first assistant to Maria Schneider. Sabina, along with her colleague Rita, now rented an apartment at Klagenfurt Straße, Villach. After some time, both of them shifted to 35, Italiener-Strasse, which was close to Wombard, a covered swimming complex, where both of them spent a lot of their spare time. Sabina loved swimming, and Wombard was the right place for her.

At work, Sabina became instrumental in resolving old, unresolved cases that had reached a dead end and had subsequently been shelved by the Police Investigating Team. Sabina had come up with the idea of circulating photographs of the dead victims in prisons all across Austria, Croatia and Germany. The idea was that convicts may link a photograph with a criminal known to them. Maria Schneider, her boss, had shelved the idea at first, but later, when Sabina suggested that they should print the photographs on playing cards, which may perhaps lead to some bored poker player in a prison recognizing a victim and coming forward with some information about the real culprit, she agreed. Maria got the playing cards distributed in prisons across Austria and to everyone's astonishment, a murder case from twenty years ago was solved with the help of an eyewitness who was lodged in prison and had volunteered to become a witness in the case.

It so happened that while playing cards, the prisoner had realized that the photograph on the card was a victim of one of his friends. His friend had told him, in confidence, about a murder that he had committed in the Faakersee, near Villach.

Based upon his statement, the case was reopened, and the culprit, who had become the owner of a Mexican restaurant at Hauptplatz, Klagenfurt, was booked on charges of murder. He was eventually convicted for life, and an unsolved case was thus solved. Sabina's law firm got a lot of publicity for the same. Maria was all over the newspapers and was thanked by the press for solving an old murder case and bringing justice to the victims' families.

In another case, going back years to 2005, a woman called Susan Walter had been shot and strangled in her home in Salzburg. The case was a dead end, and despite investigations, the police could not come up with any possible motive or suspect. There were no fingerprints or any other clues left by the killer. The police, after coming to a dead end, had closed the file for good.

Sabina was smart enough to realize that prisons were filled with convicts who very likely had connections in the crime world. They often knew certain things that the police or prosecuting authorities would never manage to find out. And sure enough, one convict recognized Susan's face on a playing card and cut a deal to reveal what he knew in exchange for money.

The law firm set about studying the files and examining the evidence. It was with the eyewitness account of the convict that they managed to apprehend the real killer: Susan's sixty-one-year-old neighbour. The convict who shared this information was, at that time, a sixteen-year-old boy and an eyewitness to the murder. He had been terrified into silence by the killer who threatened to kill him too. Now, himself facing a seven-year prison sentence for a crime he had committed, he claimed he was no longer scared of such threats and was willing to make a deal and come forth as a witness. His testimony helped resolve the case. In turn, the witness was granted leave on parole, in accordance with Austrian laws.

By now, Sabina had become the blue-eyed law assistant of Maria, as similar unsolved cases coming their way were getting solved, and the legal fees were pouring in from all corners. The Ministry of Law also expressed its appreciation for the work done by her law firm. Sabina, instead of going back to India, had applied for an extension of visa for two years and, due to Maria's help, had even obtained it from the Austrian government.

Time passed, and Sabina learnt the tricks of the trade. Once while working in her office, Sabina noticed several police cars moving towards the nearby Holiday Inn Hotel. Many people had gathered near the Holiday Inn during the holiday. Someone from her office informed her that a murder had taken place on the street behind the hotel. The incident had taken place on the pavement beside the Drava

River. Alexander Andolini, a renowned and wealthy Italian artist, had been caught red-handed with a knife soaked in blood. Murder in the peaceful town of Villach was a very rare occurrence. The killer had been caught red-handed, and it was an open-and-shut case.

Sabina tried to piece together the bits and pieces of information that poured in. Alexander was a resident of Florence, Italy, and had come to Villach to exhibit his artwork in the banquet hall of the hotel. He had gone for a stroll with his marketing assistant, Martha, on the pavement beside Drava River. After an alleged altercation with her, he had killed her in cold blood. The estimated time of death was around 10:30 p.m. No one seemed to have been around when it happened. The police had confiscated the knife to unearth what had transpired at the scene of the gory murder. Fingerprints on the knife matched those of the artist. Alexander had been arrested, and the court had remanded him to judicial custody for a fortnight.

The next morning, when Sabina entered the office, she was immediately summoned to the conference room by her boss. Her firm had been appointed as the lawyers to represent Alexander Andolini, who claimed that he had not committed the gruesome murder. Alexander's lawyers had flown in from Florence, and they needed the help and support of a local law firm such as theirs. Alexander was known to be an eccentric and sensitive artist who lost his cool quite often. He had no knowledge of the German language and spoke fluent Italian. An interpreter was required in the matter. Alexander Andolini could understand a little bit of English and converse in the same.

When Sabina walked in, she saw at least ten lawyers sitting in the conference room and discussing the case. The story was on the front page of all the newspapers. The media reported that Villach had a 0 per cent crime rate, and a gory murder was unprecedented in a that peaceful city. Further details were also reported: Mr Alexander was a renowned artist from Florence and had held an exhibition of his artwork in the hotel from 4 p.m. to 8 p.m. After having dinner in the restaurant along with his assistant, Martha, he'd gone out for a walk with her along the Drava River. The lone witness in the restaurant, Lagana at Holiday Inn, had vouched that an argument had taken place between Alexander and his assistant over some price issues. At that hour, the restaurant was practically deserted, and so was the pavement next to the Drava River.

Around 10:30 p.m., someone passing by had seen the sculptor holding a knife in his right hand and Martha lying in a pool of blood on the pavement. He had called up the police from a telephone booth, and within minutes, the police had apprehended Alexander, who was accused of committing murder. He was charged with culpable homicide under the Austrian Criminal Code. Charges were framed that provided for a death sentence or life imprisonment if found guilty. The post-mortem showed that the dagger thrust had punctured her heart, and she had died instantaneously.

The police station was located just behind Goldeness Mayor, a restaurant across the river at the Hauptplatz. The waiter from the Holiday Inn restaurant had stated to the police that there was indeed an altercation between the two at the dining table. He had also confirmed that it was Alexander who had asked Martha to accompany him for a walk to sort out the issues between them. They were seen leaving the restaurant, which was on the ground floor of the hotel, and walking towards the picturesque Drava River. No one seemed to know exactly what had happened after that. But the most crucial evidence against Alexander Andolini was the weapon used in the killing of Martha. The weapon was a knife with a marking of the Holiday Inn hotel. The prosecution had also produced an affidavit of a witness named Gerald Schonon, who had seen Alexander committing the crime. The case against the alleged murderer was indeed an open-and-shut case on account of all the evidence that was piling up.

Sabina listened to the discussions in silence. Her job was to jot down the proceedings of the meeting. Mr Renaldo, the lawyer from Florence, had met Alexander in prison. He told the lawyers present in the conference room that Alexander had pleaded innocence. Alexander had no idea how a knife, which he might have used for eating a chicken schnitzel dish at Lagana restaurant, had come into his hands when Martha was stabbed. He did not remember carrying a knife with him from the restaurant when both of them had set out for the walk.

It was eventually decided that a bail application would be prepared and an appeal would be filed before the Court when the prosecution sought further custody. Arguments were tendered by lawyers, but being such a sensitive case, Alexander was remanded to judicial custody for another fortnight by the Hon'ble Court at Vienna.

Sabina was assigned the task of preparing the rejoinder to the charge sheet prepared by the prosecution. Another application for granting bail was moved by Sabina under the guidance of Maria Schneider. However, the judge refused to grant bail after hearing the account of the eyewitness Gerald Schonon. As there was no evidence to prove the innocence of the accused, the court ruled that Alexander would remain in judicial custody during the pendency of the case.

Maria discreetly made certain enquiries and before long began to sense that there was something suspicious about Schonon's account and that he could be a man arranged by 'prison brokers'. This was the first time Sabina had heard of this term. Maria explained to her that there were prison brokers in Europe who would arrange for false witnesses for a fee.

Something was not quite right. Sabina found evidence that the eyewitness had indeed been arranged by a 'prison broker'. Her investigation revealed that Schonon was serving a prison sentence of five years for committing bank fraud in a nearby town and was in Villach, on parole, when the crime had taken place. On hearing this, Maria threw her hands up in exasperation, 'So now we have prison brokers coming to the aid of the prosecution.' Maria took it upon herself to explain this finding to the Court. This system was commonly used in Europe to conceal the source of supply. Even though it was illegal, the prosecution followed the same procedure to convict the accused and claim success in the case.

Maria Schneider, the astute lawyer, opposed the custody and argued before the judge vehemently. She argued, 'Your Honour, such sneaky arrangements often convert the case into a case of erroneous sentences. Prison brokers arrange for an incarcerated inmate to give a witness account on the side of the prosecution to achieve an indictment. In this case, a prison broker has most likely been arranged as a false witness,' she asserted.

Sabina and Maria filed another bail application in light of these facts. Arguments went back and forth. The bail application was again dismissed. Alexander was transported to the central prison in Vienna. No appeals from the Italian ambassador could help. The court, in order to put to rest the public outcry, listed the case for day-to-day hearing and, after deliberations, ruled against the accused, giving him a death sentence. The court believed that he had intentionally stolen the knife from the hotel's cutlery and planned the gruesome murder. Everything went against him, and he finally had to face the death sentence. Death by lethal injection was the final verdict given to him. The courts seldom gave the death penalty, but a foreigner committing a planned, first-degree murder on their soil was not acceptable to the division bench.

Their only hope now was to file an appeal before the High Court at Vienna. When the case was listed, Maria made the argument that the accused, Alexander, suffered from Alzheimer's Disease. She produced medical evidence to support that, and argued that a man suffering from a mental disease cannot be held accountable for his actions. The appeal fell on deaf ears. An innocent woman had been killed and the accused was to be held accountable. It seemed to be a case of fait accompli. The high court dismissed the petition. The famous artist from Florence was to face the gallows on the 19 September 2020. Maria moved a clemency petition to the President of Austria, which too was dismissed on 14 September 2020. Newspapers reported that the next five days were the last days of the culprit. News of the case was splashed across the headlines and became the talk of the town.

As Sabina was looking at the bearded face of the artist on the front page of the newspapers, her mother called from India. Sabina had not noticed that her mother had called her for the seventh time when she had eventually picked up. That was quite odd for her. But she was dejected at losing her first ever murder case, and Sabina told her mother about the imminent death of her client, which was scheduled for 5 p.m., five days later. Her mother told her that news of the sensational murder by an artist was all over the TV channels. She also asked Sabina to mail her the photographs of the accused so she could have a closer look. Sabina mailed her the newspaper photographs of the accused, though she wondered why her mother was keen on taking a closer look at the accused, Alexander Andolini, of Italian descent.

Barely five minutes later, her mother called her back. She was speaking in a high, excited tone and what she said left Sabina stunned. Her mother exclaimed, 'Sabina, I looked closely at the photographs you sent me and the ones on CNN; this artist has a striking resemblance to your father. When you first showed me his photograph on the phone, I had a strange feeling. Twenty years may have passed but I do remember your father's face. A wife can surely recognize her husband even after a lapse of twenty years.'

Sabina sat back in her chair, dumbfounded, 'But Mother, his name is Alexander Andolini. He's a resident of Florence. I've seen his passport. He's never ever hinted that he has a connection with India. I've never met him in person but how could he possibly be my father? Mother, he speaks Italian fluently. I think you are mistaken. Isn't it true that there are at least seven people on this Earth who somehow resemble each other?'

'If your father would have been alive, he would be about the same age as this person,' her mother pleaded with her. 'He would look exactly like the person in this photograph. Sabina, please try to meet him. Don't let him just die without finding out. I may be repeating myself, but a wife can indeed recognize her husband even after so many years. I will send you your father's photograph. Please visit him. Please do what I ask.' Sabina realized her mother was weeping and she consoled her by saying, 'Fine, mother, please don't cry. I will do whatever I can, although it's almost impossible to meet someone who is to be put to death five days from now.'

Just then Maria walked into the room and saw Sabina with a shocked expression on her face. When Sabina told her what her mother had said, Maria exclaimed, 'Goodness. What are you saying? How can that be possible? It's unbelievable. I met him when he was in police custody. His dialect is very much Italian. There is not an iota of evidence that he is an Indian. He is the sole inheritor of huge properties and funds from his Italian father. What gibberish are you talking about? Do not be foolish Sabina.'

Still, Sabina requested some time to further investigate the matter. Maria patted her shoulder and said, 'Go ahead and investigate as much as you want. But remember we only have a few days to save him. What is in your mind and how do you plan to take the rabbit out of the hat?'

Sabina replied sternly, 'Ma'am the past cannot be changed but the present is still in our hands. Let us assume that our client is innocent. That would mean either Alexander is the culprit or someone came from Florence to Villach at or around the same time the murder took place. I would first go through the list of all passengers who had travelled to Villach on that fateful day. My friend Rita, who knows someone in the ÖBB Railways, will help me. It may not lead to anything but it would be a beginning. I know, ma'am, it is indeed a shot in the dark but please allow me to forge ahead and investigate.'

Maria reluctantly agreed, but said, 'Look, I think this time we are barking up the wrong tree, and the chances of failure are high.' However, intense investigation resulted in a lead that was nothing short of a miracle. On the fifth day, i.e. 19 September, Sabina rushed into Maria's office, her voice high with intensity: 'Ma'am, we have to make an immediate appeal to the court to delay the execution which is slated for 5 p.m. today.'

She continued speaking in an excited tone. 'There has been a new development in the case. Martha's husband had also been in Villach on the night of the murder. No one had known this, and it was only on going through the names of every passenger on the train reaching Villach that this information was revealed. Could it have been a coincidence? Something tells me it is not.'

Sabina continued in a high tone, 'Rita's contact found out that Martha's husband had travelled by air to Venice, and then taken an ÖBB train from Venice to Villach Hauptbahnhof. It takes about three hours to reach Villach from Venice. After further checking, she found that he had indeed travelled to Villach by train on the day of the murder and taken the midnight train back from Villach to Venice. How would you explain his coming to Villach, meeting no one and leaving by midnight on the same day? Intriguing? Nor did he come back to meet the police or the prosecution lawyers after the public announcement of his wife's murder. Is that not strange behaviour? Did anyone think of calling him for testimony?' She quipped. Sabina shared all this information breathlessly with Maria, 'Shouldn't he have visited Villach at least once during the trial? After all, it was his wife who had been murdered and Alexander Andolini was already accused of being the murderer. Something about his absence just doesn't sit right.' Maria said, 'Sabina, do not forget, he did come for half a day after the autopsy to perform his wife's last rites but left soon after, on the pretext of having to look after his ailing mother.'

This sensational information had opened up another line of enquiry. Quickly, Sabina prepared an application to stop the execution till the doubts about the new turn of events were cleared. However, when Maria and Sabina appeared before the judge, he simply refused to listen as it was too late in the day. This came as a shock to Sabina. She was close to unearthing the truth and killing two birds with one stone. She could save an innocent man from death and find out whether the accused was indeed her father or not. Sabina should have allowed her senior partner to plead but she was emotionally charged. She got up and said, 'Your Honour, you are committing a grave error by dismissing this application. The presence of Martha's husband on the same night raises a genuine concern. He indeed left without meeting anyone. It is a matter of life and death. Your Honour, what if Martha was killed by her husband? What if an innocent man is being put to death for a crime he did not commit? That would tantamount to grave injustice.'

The judge was not amused by this intervention. He stated in open court, 'Senior Counsel, you must restrain your juniors to speak out of turn in the court. She is surely missing the point. Her husband might have come to meet her and on finding her murdered he might have gone back to avoid police questioning and harassment. If I was in his place, I would have done the same. Sometimes you have to eat your own words, chew your ego, swallow your pride and accept that you are wrong. I impose a fine of one thousand euros on your junior for contempt and unbecoming intervention.' Addressing Sabina, he also added, 'Remember, silence is the fence around wisdom. If your foot slips you can regain your balance but if your tongue slips you can be held guilty of conduct and contempt of court with cost. It is only a gimmick by the lawyers to buy some more time. Case dismissed with costs.'

Maria and Sabina, in utter disappointment, rushed to the prison cell and tried to persuade the Superintendent to hold off the execution given the new information that had come to light in the case. However, court orders had to be followed; two lawyers had no locus standi to halt the execution. The dishevelled, haggard-looking Alexander Andolini was brought to the execution cell and tied to a chair. Preparations were on to administer the lethal injection to him at exactly 5 p.m. This was the first time that Sabina was seeing him face-to-face. There were only two minutes left for the execution when her phone beeped and she received the photograph of her father. She had only a vague memory of her father. The photograph indeed had a striking resemblance to the accused sitting on the execution chair with his hands tied and awaiting death.

A glass barrier separated the witnesses who were required to be present at the execution from the execution cell. Sabina showed the photograph to the Superintendent and requested him to show it to the accused. Time was running out. In a few minutes, it would be too late.

After an initial no, the Superintendent reluctantly agreed and took the phone from her hands and took it to the execution room where Alexander was sitting tied to a chair. Alexander was in a pensive mood. When he saw the photograph, he requested to meet the person who had sent it. It was his last request before the lethal injection was to be administered to him. Hardly any time was left but the Superintendent could not refuse the accused his last request.

Sabina entered the execution cell. Two doctors, one nurse and two policemen were standing next to the execution chair. Sabina questioned, 'Who are you?' He said, his voice weak and barely audible, 'Why are you showing this photograph to me?' Sabina said, 'This is a photograph just sent by my mother from India. It has a striking resemblance to you, sir. Are you the person in this photograph? Are you, my father?' Her voice was heavy with emotion and trembling as she asked, 'Are you, in fact, Gulshan Ramani from India somehow masquerading as Alexander?'

'Father? Are you crazy? I have never visited India in my life. I was born and brought up in Florence. That's what my father told me. How can I be your father?' His voice was still feeble but a little clearer this time.

'Sir, just like you, my father was an artist and a sculptor.

He had a mental disorder...' Her voice trailed away hopelessly. Just then the phone rang. It was her mother. 'Sabina, did you meet him? I am certain he is your father. Please call me after meeting him,' she said in Hindi, all in one breath. The Superintendent intervened authoritatively, 'It's five o'clock. Please leave, Counsel. There can be no further delay in the execution.'

Alexander said softly: 'It's time for me to go. Please leave, *beta. Ab tum jao.*' 'Beta? Jao?' Sabina turned to him in disbelief. 'What did you say, sir? Beta?' That is a Hindi word from my native country and so is 'Ab tum jao.' But you said you were born and brought up in Florence? How could you know these words? Parents in India call their children 'beta'. I heard that Hindi word coming from your mouth loud and clear, dad,' Sabina said, starting to weep inconsolably.

'I…I don't know, but when you were talking to someone on the phone in your language, I felt that I had heard it before. I am struggling to remember and I am unable to recollect anything, anything at all, beta.'

Sabina's eyes shone. 'Sir, so you are indeed my father. Now I know it for sure. Due to acute bouts of Alzheimer's Disease, you left India and somehow reached Florence. An artist plagued with Alzheimer's and this resemblance. It can't be two different people.' Tears were rolling down her face. Alexander still seemed confused. But the officials had a job to perform.

She was ushered out of the execution cell and the doctor started administering the lethal injection to the accused. As it happened, they tried to locate a vein to give him the injection but couldn't find one. The nurse intervened and tried to find a vein again and again, but to no avail. Blood came oozing out from the arm of the accused, Gulshan Ramani, alias Alexander Andolini, whilst he was writhing in pain.

Seeing this, Senior Counsel Maria intervened, 'This is torture, sir,' she spoke to the Superintendent with an air of authority. 'I invoke the Fifth Amendment and the case of Graham vs Graham where the apex court had held that an accused facing death row cannot be tortured. If you cannot find a vein, then you must consider the other option: death by electric shock. You must stop this torture or face the judge tomorrow morning.' Maria was buying time, but was firm in her argument.

The Superintendent knew the case of 'Graham vs Graham' and he ordered for the execution to be delayed by forty-eight hours till they could make arrangements for an electric chair. If the lethal injection failed, the law provided for death by electric chair. He had gained a lease on life for another forty-eight hours. Forty-eight hours only and that was it. Maria pulled the weeping Sabina aside and said, 'Let's race down to our office and do our best in the next forty-eight hours. Sabina, you must pull yourself up. Life is like a race between cat and rat, but it is the rat who mostly wins because cat runs for food while the rat runs for its life. Let us try and save your father. No time to shed tears. Let's go and file a petition before the apex court.'

Maria and Sabina rushed to their office. They had just bought themselves some time but not too much. There was a lot to be done. A subpoena was sent on urgent basis to Florence asking the husband of the deceased Martha appear in the Court. Maria asked Sabina to first collect evidence from

Florence and then later cross-examine Benito and Gerald. Sabina Ramani had to save Gulshan Ramani. Maria advised her, 'Sabina, challenges make you more responsible and life without struggle is a life without success. Do not ever give up and learn to never quit.' Sabina took a flight to Florence and in very short time collected what she had aimed for. This time the apex court was packed with reporters and the media was covering every argument in the case. There was a high level of international interest in the proceedings. Sabina requested Maria to allow her to argue on the matter. In court, she grilled the ex-husband with thoroughness and a passion that came from her personal interest in the case. She questioned Martha's husband, 'Sir, tell me if you had come to meet your wife, then why did you purchase the return ticket for that night only? Why did you intentionally hide your first ever visit to Villach?'

Martha's husband replied, 'I had to look after my ailing mother and had no time to stay longer than required. When I found out that she had been murdered, in order to avoid police questioning and unnecessary wastage of time, money and energy, I left for Florence.'

Sabina raised her voice, 'What would you have achieved in barely a few hours if you stayed in Villach? What was the urgency for you to come all the way from Florence to meet her? Moreover, the medical report of your mother, which I am holding in my hand, shows that she has no such ailment as you claim. And please tell me who this woman called Florentine is. She is supposed to be close to you. Is infidelity a reason for you to murder the victim? I accuse you of committing the crime. Mr Alexander Andolini is innocent while you are the real culprit.'

He replied, 'There is no false claim. My mother is seriously ill and I could not have left her alone for a long time. I do not know any women by the name of Florentine at all. Your accusations are malicious to the core.'

Sabina quipped, 'Are you sure? I have a photograph of you with her. And what about the millions of liras that you owe to the Cupid Casino in Florence? You have lost millions in gambling and only the insurance money to be received after the demise of Martha could save you.' She produced evidence and he indeed was caught unaware. 'We have an eyewitness in the court that saw you stealing the knife from Lagana restaurant at Holiday Inn and then following Alexander and Martha while they were walking on the pavement next to Drava River. The witness also says that you suddenly overtook them and without any altercation or provocation stabbed Martha twice. Your motive was crystal clear: hitting three birds with a stone. Firstly, killing your wife to pave way for your relationship with Florentine. Of course, Martha was the main hurdle. Secondly, getting her insurance money to pay off the debts, and, last but not the least, the indictment of Alexander Andolioni, whom you despised the most.' To the court, she said, 'Here is the certificate which proves that he owes millions of liras to the casino at Florence. I am placing it as "Exhibit 1". A photograph of the lovey-dovey couple is also being filed.'

The evidence was accumulating against the accused. Eventually, the husband broke down under the pressure of her valid and sustained questioning. He confessed that he had a suspicion that his wife was having an extramarital affair with Alexander. There was also something more to the matter. Martha had been insured for a hefty sum. Alexander Andolini was bearing the premium. Moreover, he admitted to having been in a relationship with another woman known as Florentine. All these matters led him to plan the murder. He had gone into the kitchen of Holiday Inn and stolen the murder weapon from there without anybody noticing the theft, or that's what he had thought at that time.

There was a big uproar in the court following this revelation. Sabina explained that prison brokers may have arranged the eyewitness. 'Your Honour, there are prison brokers who convince newly jailed convicts to become eyewitnesses in sensitive or complicated cases in exchange for a fee.' She went on, 'The prosecution could not establish mens rea or any motive for Mr Gulshan Ramani, alias Alexander Andolini, killing the victim. He might have been suffering from a bout of Alzheimer's Disease and was confused about where he was, what he was doing or how the knife came into his hand. I am also sure that Martha's husband had a completely wrong notion about his wife having an affair with her boss. Most likely, she was just being sympathetic to him, which the killer misinterpreted as an affair. And now the new angle of the relationship which he has with another woman gives him the motive to kill Martha. Your Honour, since he has admitted to having murdered his wife, my client is innocent. An order for his release must be passed before he is put on an electric chair within the next few hours.'

She went on to explain the modus operandi of the prison brokers: 'Prison brokers, in connivance with the police, secretly take the so-called eyewitnesses to the scene of the crime and meticulously prepare them to give evidence against the accused to clinch a case. There is a massive fee involved for doing this. At times they are given long-term parole by the prosecutors.

'Your Honour, it is a known fact that by finding an eyewitness, the police and prosecution save a lot of time, money, energy, legal fees, investigation expenses, and so on. Moreover, the police personnel in charge get promoted for solving high-profile cases. It is a well-known secret that investigating authorities keep aside some funds to buy such eyewitnesses through the services of these prison brokers.'

'Your Honour, in all likelihood, the same thing happened here as well. Prison brokers were used by the police to nail the accused who was found holding the knife in one hand. So, even though there was no mens rea, nobody thought about investigating her husband who turned out to be the actual killer. They all heard and believed the witness Gerald Schonon, who was arranged by the prison brokers to convict Alexander, all for a fee.'

'Your Honour,' she continued, 'in such cases not only do the prison brokers receive a fee but the so-called eyewitness is also released on parole. Later, as a reward, his sentence is reduced due to "good behaviour". There are deals made all through the system and everyone gets a cut. These prison brokers are at large and because it is a question of life and death, they can make huge amounts by arranging witnesses for the prosecution as well as the defence.'

'I rest my case, Your Honour. Would you request the Hon'ble Court to pass an order for the immediate release of Alexander Andolini and issue summons to the prison broker. Enrich Bernard, and his stooge, Gerald Schonon?' she said triumphantly. The judge passed an order to grant an interim stay on the execution of the accused, Alexander, till a final order was passed. Alexander Andolini, alias Gulshan Ramani, father of Sabina Ramani, was thus granted a reprieve by the High Court. The order for his execution was rescinded. Sabina immediately left for the prison, leaving the court proceedings to her senior. When she reached the prison, she found her father tied to the electric chair. The executioner was about to press the button when Sabina entered and yelled at the top of her voice, '*Stoppen Sie die Ausführung* (Stop the execution).' She had arrived at the nick of time to save her father from imminent death.

Subsequently Enrich Bernald was summoned to the court and confessed that there was in fact no eyewitness to the crime supposedly committed by Alexander Andolini. It had all been falsely brokered by him through a prisoner named Gerald Schonon. This was a quid pro quo matter. Once again, the court went into an uproar.

Sabina took a copy of the order. News coverage of the prison broking scandal had been shooting TRP ratings of the TV channels to new heights. Now the verdict created an even more frenzied media response: An innocent artist had almost been given a lethal injection and had been pulled back minutes before from the jaws of death by a young counsel who turned out to be his daughter, the TV channels were collectively exclaiming.

Subsequently the judge not only discharged the innocent artist facing death row but passed strict judgements against the erring police and government officers. The prison broker Enrich Bernard was arrested and charged.

Meanwhile, Sabina had called her mother to Austria to meet her long-lost husband. Rashmi was now meeting her husband after a gap of twenty years. Sabina's mother Rashmi had carried all the photographs she could find of her time spent with Gulshan. When husband and wife met, they both had tears in their eyes and for a long time, they could not speak. When Rashmi showed him the old photographs of their wedding, his memory seemed to get revived temporally. It was an emotional moment for the entire family.

By now, Alexander, the rich and renowned artist from Florence, was convinced that he was none other than Gulshan, or Gul, as he was known to his close friends. He flew back with Sabina and Rashmi to his native country where he met all his relatives and friends though it was difficult for him to remember all of them.

And then a miracle happened. While visiting Birla Mandir near his old house he suddenly remembered that there was a ridge forest behind the temple and there was a cave in the park next to the temple. He recalled that as a child he would sit on animals made of stone—a camel, an alligator, an elephant—in front of a cave. When he saw these stone animals, his memory came back in a flash. It all came back: his school, his art college, his parents, even his close friends in the college.

He asked his wife and daughter to select the place where they wanted to stay. He was wealthy. He could buy them a big mansion anywhere they wanted. Both Rashmi and Sabina instead chose to stay in India and Gulshan agreed to shift from Italy to spend the rest of his life in New Delhi with his family. His son had grown to be a handsome young man and he was an IIT engineer working in a modest IT firm in Gurgaon. For the first time, the family was wealthy. For the first time, after twenty years, there was a homecoming.

Maria Schneider saw to it that the system of false witnesses arranged by the prison brokers came to an end. A promulgation order was passed against it by the Government. The system of arranging for witnesses by prison brokers came to an end. Soon Sabina received a call from Nikhil.

She was thoroughly enjoying the love and affection showered by her father upon her. Nevertheless, she waited impatiently for Nikhil Chopra to land at New Delhi International Airport.

When the plane landed at Terminal 3, she was anxious but had a smile on her lips. Who knows what may happen next or what was in store for her and Nikhil Chopra? Life of late, as it had been, had been full of surprises, and they had all been amazing.

VAZRA FALLS

Excitement was at its peak when four friends from Bangalore, all brilliant engineers from IT companies, landed at Goa's Dabolim Airport on Indigo flight 6E–6533. All of them were staying in the vicinity of Purvankara Seasons Residential Complex, Bangalore. They had become friendly with each other after having met at the club situated near the E Block Tower. All of them were enthusiasts, full of energy and in their late twenties. Being neighbours, they used to meet more often. The four couples were like-minded as they enjoyed each other's company. Last month itself, they had been to Wellington and Ooty for a sojourn and had enjoyed the trip thoroughly.

This time, their purpose was not to laze around on the beautiful beaches of North and South Goa and gulp down a few alcoholic drinks. On the contrary, they had booked themselves an adventurous trip to Vazra Waterfalls situated near the north-eastern part of the Goa-Karnataka border.

Their plane had taken off and landed at the scheduled time. Two vehicles were waiting for them near Gate No. 2, where a casino sign flashed time and again. The four couples left for the jungle resort straightaway, where stunning landscape in all in its vibrant form awaited them. The destination was known as 'Wild Beast Resort', and it was suitable for adventurous people who wanted to hike through the narrow paths to the beautiful Vazra Waterfalls. The Wild Beast Resort boasted an infinity pool and wilderness, where one could listen intermittently to the chords of nature.

They reached the platform of the resort situated at base level by 9:30 p.m., from where they would have to take the rope-way to Wild Beast Resort. The resort was in complete wilderness, situated on a mountaintop with a breathtaking view. All eight of them, Namit-Riya, Mohit-Ashu, Shantanu-Sharmila, and Raman-Rati, were dog-tired and hit their beds in their respective cottages assigned to them by the ever energetic and agile Namdev. Namdev was the co-coordinator for guests. Namdev was of average height but stout build, with a twirling moustache and a strange beard. It was a mixture of a trencher beard and a moustache grown by Mexicans. He always swore, bidding Mohit and Ashu adieu. The four cottages allotted to them were well-furnished and comfortable.

There were two famous falls in the mountainous region—Pandava Falls and Vazra Falls. The hilly trek to the Pandava Falls was supposed to begin at precisely 7 a.m. the next morning. That was the routine followed by the management for the last three years of its existence. It was a place with facilities. The jungle density was at its peak within the area covered by the resort. Unknown to the visitors, they had put up certain nets at strategic points so that predators lurking around could not enter the resort area and disturb the guests.

It was a unique experience. Securing accommodation at Wild Beast Resort was difficult.

While Namit and Riya had married two years earlier and had been contemplating having children, Mohit and Ashu had a three-year-old daughter. Namit and Mohit worked at a software company, handling the supply chain for its semiconductor products. Ashu had left her three-year-old daughter with her parents before embarking on the trip. While Namit was of average height, Mohit was the tallest amongst them. He was the strongest of the lot, some six feet two inches tall and burly. Shantanu and Sharmila were dark-skinned and thin. Namit and Riya were of average height, and both were on the bulky side.

Shantanu and Sharmila originally hailed from Kolkata, having shifted to Bangalore just six months back. They were in a live-in relationship and were not yet married. Sharmila wanted to assess her boyfriend, before tying the proverbial nuptial knot.

Raman and Rati had been working as software engineers at a real estate company in Gurgaon, near New Delhi, and had shifted to Bangalore about a year ago. Ashu was a housewife and had opted to nurture her daughter; all the others were working in one capacity or another in the busy IT city of Bengaluru.

Mohit and Ashu, being early risers, were comfortably sipping coffee sitting in the two chairs on the balcony and admiring the beauty of nature. The trek was still a good two hours away. Ashu whispered to Mohit so that her voice would not carry to Shantanu and Sharmila's balcony. 'Hey Mohit, can you feel the vibrancy in this paradise called Wild

Beast Resort? Can you hear the calls made by a male sambar? One can really experience pure tranquillity and comfort in this natural realm.'

'Yes, Ashu, you are damn right,' Mohit replied excitedly. 'I, too, am astonished at the picturesque settings and the serene surroundings overlooking the Panda Valley down below. And look over there, the hundred-metre fall, known as Vazra Falls. Isn't it panoramic and beautiful?' They were admiring the beauty of nature when the doorbell rang, and the ever-effervescent Namdev stood there holding two cups of tea with some ginger cookies. Ashu was surprised but equally flattered by the service that early in the day. 'Madam, there are exquisite arrangements for tea and coffee in this cottage itself, but when I saw you on the balcony, I thought of getting hot cups of tea for both of you. I am and shall always be at your service, Madam,' Namdev said as he bowed before Ashu. Mohit came from behind and, while thanking him, slipped a hundred-rupee note in Namdev's open palm as a tip. Once the crisp currency note was passed on, it vanished from the palm in seconds.

Namdev smiled with a wide grin as if Mohit had saved his life. Showing his brown teeth, he smiled on seeing the hundred-rupee currency note. Ashu stopped him by asking, 'Namdev, err, that's what your name is, right? Are these the only cottages that have such a beautiful view or are there some others as well?'

'Ma'am, there are thirteen cottages, including the twin cottages of the owner, which have a built-in swimming pool,' he replied with a wide grin. Mohit intervened, 'Namdev, isn't thirteen supposed to be an unlucky number? Why would the owner keep thirteen cottages in the resorts if he could avoid having cottage no. 13?'

Namdev replied, 'Sir, not for our master Vikram, alias Vicky, who is the owner of this resort. Everything connected with thirteen is lucky for him. He was born on 13 September. All his flashy cars have thirteen on their registration plates. Sir, it is here, in this sprawling, thirteen-acre, hilly resort with flowing cascades and nature therapy that youths like you are pampered. Our owner, Vicky Sahib, feels that we share with our esteemed guests, nature in its most magical form.'

Ashu nodded, fully agreeing with him, 'Namdev, I bet your master, Vicky, must be a nature lover to have done so much in this godforsaken forest. Even I do not believe in numbers being lucky or unlucky. If you work hard and have a vision, you are bound to succeed.'

Namdev replied with an expression of pride, 'Yes, ma'am, he often says with a tinge of pride, that by fusing the elements of natural space and aesthetically eco-friendly architecture, he has created subtle surprises, vibrant forms and mystical charms. He really admires the sunrise beyond those hills, and as such it is a successful venture, madam.' He continued unabashedly, 'Ma'am, being in the realm of the Western Ghat forests, our trained guides, especially Mike Braganza, will invite you to join him on the nature trek up to the Pandava or Vazra waterfalls. He will certainly take you to the specially designed hideaways, which offer the very essence of living in nature and of utmost peace, solitude and tranquillity. We also have Robin Merchant here, a well-known herpetologist. He studies the forest and imparts his knowledge about the different species dwelling in this forest every evening at 8 p.m. *Mademoiselle, comment tallez-vous*?' Mohit intervened, 'Oh! So, you can speak in French too! Namdev, you certainly have a flair for other languages.'

Namdev said, 'Sir, I know at least ten languages. Most of the guests are foreigners. They love the treacherous, albeit adventurous, trek to the Pandava or Vazra Falls, replete with wild beasts, and hence the name of the resort. At various entry points, large nets have been installed to prevent predators from entering the resort or the trekking path. Mike Braganza often says, "Travel light if you want to fly, giving up everything that weighs you down."'

'Thanks for all the information, Namdev, but what Braganza says also has a different philosophical meaning,' Mohit said while closing the door. Mohit was wondering why Namdev, who was all hung up about the picturesque resort, had described the trek as treacherous. It was typical of Namdev, who did not budge an inch till he received his tip from his honoured guests. He appeared from nowhere and disappeared to nowhere after his palm got greased by money.

By 7 a.m., all the couples, along with three other foreigners from Sweden, had gathered at the reception to undertake the one-hour trek to the Pandava Falls. All of them were given a rope by Mr Mike Braganza—the guide and leader of the trek. They had to tie the same around their upper torso, lest they slip while trekking along some of the narrowest paths leading to the waterfalls. The Pandava waterfall was in fact an hour away from Ponda City in Goa. Everyone listened intently to the instructions provided by Mr Braganza. While Namit and Riya, and Shantanu and Sharmila listened to him intently, Mohit kept on cracking jokes and passing comments. However,

Mike Braganza was visibly annoyed. Speaking a bit loudly, he said, 'Mr Mohit, I hope you understand that trekking in this mountainous terrain is a tough and risky affair.'

Mohit replied with a smile, 'Sir, when things get tough, the tough get going. No issues, sir, I can handle any situation even if I am dangling in the air.' He laughed to the bemusement of other participants. Raman intervened, 'It may not turn out to be the cakewalk that you are expecting it to be. Let's pay attention to what Mr Braganza is telling us. You never know, it may come in handy.' Mike Braganza shrugged his shoulders and moved forward with a huff and started moving on the plush green trekking path.

The experienced guide continued to impart knowledge about the reptiles that infested the thick forest, and spoke uninterrupted on the mic. 'There are 140 species of birds in this forest, and at the last count in 2010, around four hundred different species of lizards, snakes and other reptiles were found in this area. Snakes fascinate all of us, even if for some that fascination amounts to terror. But for some, this fascination borders on addiction. There are three types of cobras that we have here in this forest: manacled cobra, spectacled cobra and Central Asian cobra.'

Raman and Rati were quietly following their leader and his instructions to the hilt. All were conscious of the fact that at some places, not only would the path narrow down, but there would be a deep gorge down below. One false move and it would be curtains! As a matter of abundant caution, they were tied to a rope which was strong enough to overcome any such incident. Mohit murmured, 'We are not interested in knowing about the variety of the slimy reptiles.' Braganza, though far ahead, heard it. 'Mr Mohit, I heard that comment of yours,' he said, turning around to face Mohit, who was the thirteenth trekker. Braganza continued to talk, 'This trek is surely treacherous, but it is not as tough as the Kudremukh Trek. For your information, Kumara Parvata is considered to be one of the toughest, yet, must-do treks in the Western Ghats of Karnataka. Mr Mohit, please be a tad serious.'

'I apologize for my impudence, sir, but we are not keen on knowing much about the species of snakes or whether they are hiding amongst the bushes somewhere near us. When I was studying engineering at IIT Delhi, lizards and snakes freely roamed around our college campus. I was least bothered then; I am least bothered now. I have held them with my bare hands many a time. In fact, I have killed a few of them too,' Mohit boasted. Braganza retorted, 'And what about the Indian rock python. Have you handled it too with your bare hands, sir?' he asked, a bit sarcastically. He continued, 'Sir, this largest species of snake is around 3.5 to 4 metres long and capable of devouring mammals and reptiles after squeezing them to death with its sheer strength.'

Sharmila responded to the leader and said, 'Yes, sir, rock pythons are indeed scary. They are identified by a stout, smooth-scaled, dull yellowish-white body that has prominent rock-like marks on the entire upper region, from which it derives its common name, the rock python.'

'Yes, ma'am, you are absolutely right,' quipped the guide, and turning back, resumed his walk leading to Pandava Falls. Braganza further said, 'The trek gear that we carry is not a luxury but a necessity. We are, after all, frail creatures compared to the forces of nature. The best thing is to always try and avoid getting into potentially life-threatening situations. Although, sometimes, people do get into such situations inadvertently, and then it becomes a severe challenge to come out of it without getting hurt. Five trekkers from West Bengal died after getting caught in bad weather in Sundar Dhunga.'

Braganza reminded the trekkers of the fateful incident and urged them to be careful. He said on his mic while leading from the front, 'Dear friends, treks do look easy at times but can turn fatal if not taken seriously. Two friends, Akshay and Navneet, embarked on a trek to Shikhar Devi on 5 January 2017. The Himalayas witnessed heavy snowfall around that time and nobody knew about their whereabouts for the next six days. One of them died in the snowstorm that followed. The list is endless.'

Just then, Ashu, who had lost her concentration while reprimanding Mohit, slipped and fell towards the deep gorge. She shrieked for help. While Braganza immediately grabbed on to a nearby tree as an expert would, Mohit dug his foot deep into the muddy path and tried to pull the rope upwards. Suzy, the Swedish trekker accompanying her boyfriend Alex, had lost her footing and fallen to the side. Ashu had been in front of Suzy, and Suzy's fall had led her to lose her balance too.

The two shouted for help and seemed petrified to the core. The strong rope held their weight. When Ashu looked down, she could see the landscape far below. For a moment, she thought this was going to be the end of her life.

Braganza shouted, 'Not to worry, these kinds of mishaps happen, and that's why we tie the ropes around your torso. We will pull both of you up. Please maintain your cool and stay calm. Your movements may delay the process of lifting you back on this narrow path.'

Both the girls obeyed the guide's instructions and, for the time being, forgot that they were suspended in the air. All the others helped Mohit and Braganza pull them to safety.

Ashu, on climbing back to the path, started crying and uttered, 'I don't want to go further, I have had enough, I want to go back.' Braganza paused calmly and quietened their nerves. 'Please cool down. This kind of incident does not happen often. If one is careless, it can happen. Folks, let's forget about it and move ahead. Another two hundred yards, and you will freak out at the breathtaking view of the Pandava Valley. Come, come, ma'am, let's continue our trek. The narrow path ends here only.'

Braganza turned towards Suzy and asked her, 'What about you, Suzy? Are you willing to continue?' Suzy could not reply as she was clinging to Alex and was shivering with fear. 'If Mohit and Braganza had not acted swiftly, for all you know, everybody might have gone down one by one,' quipped Raman. Braganza tried to soften them up and said, 'Sir, it has never happened. There are no recorded deaths or falls in the Pandava Falls area. Believe me, it was just a one-off incident. You will surely enjoy this trek as others have done in the past.'

Suzy was trying to control her shivering, and with great effort, she got up and got ready to resume the trek. Though visibly disturbed, they encouraged each other to move on and complete the trek to Pandava waterfalls. Braganza was right. After around two hundred yards, they were face to face with the massive waterfall. Water was pooling into a small lake and flowing downwards towards Ponda. It indeed was a breathtaking view. The trek from there onwards was flat, and most of them ran towards the lake, which had crystal clear water. They forgot about the recent happening and wanted to enjoy the view of the waterfall.

Braganza spoke a little loudly to overcome the sound emanating from the waterfall, 'Folks, it's time for a swim and to have some fun. We are all in one piece, and that's what matters. No injuries; we have emerged safely from a mishap which we have somehow overcome.'

Except Suzy, all of them changed their clothes, put on swimsuits and dived into the lake, which had clear but cold water. The lake was about eight to ten feet deep, and swimming there was fun for all of them. Mike and his helper got started on preparing the snacks for the trekkers, who would be on the shores of the beautiful lake right beneath the massive Pandava Falls.

A swim in the lake erased their memory of the recent incident, and all of them tried to enter the cave behind the waterfall. Braganza once again spoke on his mic, 'Ladies and gentlemen, around five thousand years back or so, the clans of Kauravas and Pandavas had played something like a game of poker. The Pandavas lost the game and, in turn, their fort and all of their belongings. They were exiled and based upon the bet they had to wander in the forest for thirteen long years, and in case they were found in the thirteenth year, then they would have to repeat the exile for yet another twelve years.' He paused for a while, then continued narrating the story from the Mahabharata.

'It is rumoured that to hide and remain undetected, they hid behind the Pandava Falls, in this very cave, and came down at night in search of food and to take a bath in this holy lake. They could not afford to get detected by their opponents, who were on the lookout. Pandava Falls gave them the desired protection. By hiding here for a considerable period, they were able to avoid detection till the thirteenth year of their exile,' he concluded.

Suzy enquired, 'Mr Braganza, who were these rulers of India, and why in the world would they go for such a kind of bet? What kind of games did they play?'

'You are right, Suzy,' exclaimed Braganza. 'They ruled over a large part of northern India, and these two clans were cousins with rival claims on the throne. It's a long story, but in a nutshell, a battle known as "Mahabharata", was fought, and the Kaurava clan lost. But coming back to this holy lake, this is where the Pandavas hid during their last year of exile.'

Mohit asked, 'Have you heard about the waterfall near Khajuraho Temple in Madhya Pradesh, in the midst of a forest, which is called Pandava Falls, and it is believed that they stayed there for one year while in exile. There is a Sher-e-Punjab restaurant, and another restaurant in a treetop near the Pandava Falls. They say the same story you narrated, sir. Now tell me which one to believe?' 'Why are they so famous that every place has been attached to them?' asked Alex inquisitively.

Mohit said, 'That is because thousands of people died in that battle, and sermons were delivered to the Pandavas by none other than Lord Krishna. That's why the epic was written, and another holy book, known as the Bhagavad Gita also emerged during that battle. Lord Krishna gave a sermon to the Pandavas, which became the essence of Hinduism.'

Namit, who had been quiet all this while, intervened and asked Alex, 'Sir, have you heard about Lord Krishna?'

Alex replied, 'Of course, in Bern there is a huge temple and what you call "*ashram*" of ISKCON established by Swami Prabhupad. I have attended the religious programmes over there. One of my cousins is an ardent disciple of ISKCON. He has renounced the world and become a devotee of Lord Krishna.'

Mike Braganza apologetically stated, 'Sorry Mohit, I have simply repeated whatever was told to me by the previous guide about Ponda Falls, later known as Pandava Falls. I had my doubts about it having been a hideout and that's why I used the word "rumour". It was known up till the medieval period as Pandava Falls but when the Portuguese occupied Goa in 1510, they changed the name to Ponda.'

'I understand,' Mohit replied in a soft tone. Namit said, 'Alex, we give importance to the age-old epic because it teaches a lot of things about righteousness to us. The number one being the sermon given by Lord Krishna, which is known as "Gita Gyan". From it we have also learnt that it is important to have a good adviser. The Kaurava clan had a bad advisor called Shakuni who hailed from Kandhara, Afghanistan, while the Pandavas were advised at every stage of the battle by Lord Krishna.'

Braganza told them that, but for a few bats, there was nothing in the caves, which were covered by the massive Pandava Falls. They were given twelve neatly packed snack packets containing sandwiches, cashew nuts and pastries. All of them were hungry, and they began drinking some chilled Coke.

On their way back, Braganza took a different route. While leading the trekkers, he explained on his mic, 'We are going towards the resort, but we are taking a different course. The forest is not dense, and the path moves in an unconvoluted manner. As we take a turn, however, what you will find is not mud but quicksand. You must carefully follow the leader and avoid the quicksand.'

Following their leader, the trekkers walked for some time until they reached a bend in the path. They stopped to see a gory sight. A sambar was stuck in the quicksand, and whilst squeaking, it was trying to wriggle out of it. Its neck and face were visible, while the rest of its body was submerged in the granular material. The sambar saw the trekkers and, through its innocent eyes, pleaded for help and for its life. Rati shouted, 'Sir, can't we do anything to save the poor soul?' Mike replied, 'We can, but it will need a humongous effort to save the entrapped sambar. It's a big-sized one and might have been entrapped while running from a predator. Let's hurry and throw a rope sling towards the sambar and try to pull it out of the quicksand. Otherwise, it's certain death for the creature.' All of them got together, and with a sling thrown at the sambar's neck, they tried to pull it out. The sambar writhed in pain as the rope tightened around its neck. However, the Sambar, too, was desperate to make an effort at the same time. Mike Braganza threw another rope to encircle its body, and with a heave, all of them pulled the poor animal out of the quicksand. The sambar had witnessed death from close quarters; it looked at the humans, as if expressing its gratitude, and then sped away and disappeared into the forest.

Raman and Rati jumped in ecstasy and started clapping. They had been successful in saving a life. They were zoophiles to the core and had been animal rights activists for a long time. Once the animal's life was saved, they were the happiest of the lot.

The entourage of thirteen participants walked back to the resort without any further incident. They returned by around 5 p.m. and were apprised that they could rest for an hour or so before they went to witness the sunset at the sunset point. Namdev, irrespective of the hectic trip, served coffee at the sunset point to them along with some cookies.

In the evening, at around 6:15 p.m., after they had visited the sunset point, there was a lecture by the anthropologist Robin Merchant, a Parsi in his late sixties. He had spent a major part of his life searching for species in the forest. He had written many books on these living creatures. He had also extensively researched the variety of plants and trees in the dense forests all over India.

Robin Merchant introduced himself to the audience at an amphitheatre created out of wooden logs. Before he could utter a word, Sharmila asked him, 'Sir, can I ask you a question? Are you aware of the Indian rock python swallowing humans? It is huge, around four metres in length. It is believed to have swallowed many animals, including sambars, foxes, wolves, and leopards. What about humans, sir?'

Robin grimaced and said, 'The tales of the rock python attempting to swallow humans or children, for that matter, are false, baseless and just rumours. No such attack on humans has ever happened here in this valley. However, despite their lack of threat to human life, the sheer size of the snake scares the humans in a human–python conflict situation.'

He smiled a little and further stated, 'It is rather the opposite. We try to rescue or remove a rock python when it is cornered, trapped, or injured in an area where it could pose a threat to others. It is indeed an endangered species. We do not want it to cease to exist on this planet.'

Robin continued to speak about pythons and their habits. He said, 'As far as I know, no such incident has happened here. But an Indonesian woman was killed and swallowed by a seven-metre-long python. Though such incidents are rare, they did happen in Indonesia. These Indian rock pythons are much smaller in size and are, in fact, afraid of humans. All animals, whether a python or a tiger, are literally afraid of the biggest predator on this planet—humans. Yes, humans are the biggest predators, folks,' he said emphatically. Ashu was curious and not satisfied with the assurances provided by Robin Merchant. She raised her hands, got up and asked him, 'Sir, what really happened to the Indonesian lady?'

'Well,' Robin hesitated for a moment and then said, 'Watiba, the Indonesian fifty-four-year-old woman, went missing one day while she had gone out to her vegetable garden on Muna Island in Sulawesi province in Indonesia. Her sandals and machete were found after a day. Later, a giant python with a bloated belly was found lying about a hundred metres away. I would request you not to dwell much on the subject. We are in the open, and I can see some penetrating eyes in the dense forest, which we are surrounded by, but, in the first place, I must tell you, rather inform you that no such python or any such large predator can enter this resort. You are well-protected by a net which covers the entrance. It has been placed in such a manner that no wild beast or reptile can enter this resort.'

Ashu asked him again, 'Sir, we understand that no incident of any sort has been reported in and around Wild Beast Resort. We also know that all guests and residents here are well-protected. But one more thing is true, that there can always be a first time. I don't mean to scare anybody here, but if you will kindly let us know as to how they attack and how one can protect oneself, I would be obliged.'

Somewhat reluctantly Robin replied, 'You see, reticulated pythons are at times more than ten to twelve feet in length. They ambush their prey, wrapping themselves around it tighter as it exhales. They kill either by suffocation or the victim suffers from a cardiac arrest from being squeezed. Then they swallow their food as a whole. Their jaws are connected by very flexible ligaments so that they can stretch their mouths and swallow large prey.'

Rati intervened, 'Sir, you are referring to animals, but here we are more concerned about the humans. Please do let us know a way out if such a predator attacks a human being.'

Robin looked mildly irritated, but soon calmed his nerves. He finally said, 'Look, pythons are mostly and exclusively animal feeders. They usually avoid eating humans. One reason for this is that they are scared of humans. Secondly, when they try to swallow humans, the restricting factor is the human's shoulder blades. In 2005, a Burmese python tried to swallow an alligator. It killed and swallowed the alligator, but in the process, its belly burst, and it died. But these opportunistic hunters can be surprisingly resilient too. If they cannot find suitable prey, they can live for long periods on very little food until they see something big enough to satisfy their hunger.'

He continued, 'Dear friends, the anthropologist, Thomas Headland, who spent decades in the Philippines studying the behaviour of reptiles, has claimed that since the Agata community over there is small-statured, they have been ambushed by rock pythons, but most of them have been able to fend them off using their machetes. These pythons are sensitive to vibrations and heat from lamps, and, as such, normally avoid human settlements. You may not be aware, but when we cross over our protected area and go for an hour of trekking towards the Pandava or Vazra waterfalls, we will have drummers who will always be two to three hundred yards ahead. They will keep walking and keep playing the drums. Even their soft drumming can be heard by these reptiles, who move away from the path. These reptiles do not have ears, but they can detect vibrations caused by the drumming, and they vamoose from your trekking paths.'

Namdev quickly realized that the lecture was going in the wrong direction, which could be detrimental to the resort's business. He intervened, 'Ladies and gentlemen, it is already 9:30 p.m., and we have to be at the dining hall for dinner. By 6:30 a.m. tomorrow, we have to leave for yet another enchanting tour of the stunning Vazra Falls. Please have your delicious meals and sleep well and reach the reception area by 6:30 a.m. on the morrow. Good night.'

The next morning was quite bright, and the upper rim of the sun appeared on the horizon. Rati, raising her voice, asked Namit to wake up and enjoy the beauty of nature. Riya hurriedly made two cups of tea from the in-house percolator and the tea sachets, which were neatly kept on the side table.

Riya then said again, 'Honey, let's get ready and try to reach in time for our trek to commence as scheduled.' While they were coming out of their cottage, they saw Raman and Rati moving ahead towards the meeting place. Namit waved at them, and all four walked towards the reception, where the others soon joined them. Mohit and Ashu were already in the reception area. Ashu said, 'We were the first ones to reach here. Mohit has been up and about since 4 a.m. He even went for a walk before the sun was up.'

One by one, the trekkers assembled at the reception area and had a quick bite at the well-laid buffet in the reception hall. All of them were in high spirits, looking forward to the adventure ahead.

Braganza and Namdev threw their ever-effervescent smile. Braganza spoke, 'Folks, it's a half-hour walk to the base camp. We shall stop there for some snacks. Thereafter, we will move towards the famous Vazra Falls. Keep your cameras with you since mobiles won't work here. There are no towers or Wi-Fi systems in this dense forest. It might be a little exhausting, but the joy of reaching the goal will revitalize you. When you see the Vazra Falls, the moment you witness the beauty of the water falling from the mountains, you shall forget all your exhaustion of walking and trekking through this difficult mountainous terrain.'

He was used to repeating these lines each time, and it was the good old Namdev who never showed any signs of boredom while listening. Braganza continued, 'One of the major advantages of trekking is that it improves your physical health, reduces stress and improves cardiovascular strength.

Exposure to nature can counteract the negative impacts of a stressful life.'

For some reason, Ashu and Mohit started clapping and the others followed, although it wasn't clear whether they were being ironic or not. Mohit commented, 'The information is pretty good, but I read somewhere that, most importantly, one should not go trekking with their hands in their pockets. If one falls, the hands will remain stuck in the pocket. Most trekkers, I believe, underestimate the hilly terrain and overestimate their own capabilities. While trekking, as they say, we should never overestimate our virtues and capabilities and underestimate the dangers that lie ahead.' Mike Braganza smiled and said, 'I agree with you, sir.' He then gave a signal, and the group started to move towards Vazra Falls.

All of them were moving on a narrow path when suddenly Mike Braganza signalled for them to stop. He had heard the sound of leaves rustling and had sensed that a predator might be around. He had not told the trekkers that he had heard of a forty-foot rock python having snuck into the forest in and around the trekking path to find prey. Being large, if it were not satisfied by eating rats and squirrels, it would not hesitate to eat big mammals to satisfy its hungry belly. There were walls and nets around the resort area and the trekking path, protecting trekkers from hungry pythons or other wild beasts.

All of them held their breath, and an ominous silence prevailed. Mohit whispered to Braganza, 'Sir, is there anything wrong? As it is, the weather has turned bad, and a storm is brewing. The velocity of the wind has increased tremendously, and it has started to drizzle.' Braganza warned him not to utter a word and to stay where they were. Suddenly, they froze when they saw a large rock python move towards the path where the entire group was standing. The python, on noticing the group, withdrew and slid behind the bushes. The whole entourage remained entranced for some time.

Everybody had had a glimpse of the giant python, and Ashu, Sharmila, Riya, and Rati had become completely petrified. Suzy started to shiver; a bout of anxiety had struck her. The feeling of a predator looming nearby was enough to instil fear in them. Ashu roared, 'Mr Braganza, I do not wish to continue the trek. I intend to go back to the safety of the resort, which is well-protected.'

Braganza replied in the negative, 'No, madam, we will stay on the path. Do not worry; I know it was indeed scary, but rock pythons do not attack humans. Let's continue the trek. I am, in fact, carrying a machete, too. Namdev and I are capable of warding off any beast that might come near you. You are as safe here as you are in the resort. You need not worry, madam.' He reassured the trekkers, but they remained unconvinced. Mohit replied, 'Sir, I have an uncanny feeling that the predator is watching us from behind those bushes. If it is hungry enough, it may lay an ambush. Suppose it struck from behind? By the time you come to our aid, it will have devoured one of us. That's precisely what Mr Merchant had stated yesterday. Pythons ambush and encircle their prey with their tails.

Braganza spoke with concern, 'That's why I am repeatedly asking you to move forward towards Vazra Falls. No animal would attack in the open. As I said earlier, they are afraid of us.'

Namdev spoke after an eerie silence, 'As this place is too dense for my liking, just a few yards ahead, there is a slope and some open space. The reptile won't attack us in an open space. I would suggest that…' Before he could complete his sentence, the rock python struck from sideways, appearing suddenly from the bushes and wrapping itself around Rati's body. Rati shrieked, but it was done so swiftly that nobody could react instantly.

In a flash, Rati was gone. The beast had taken her behind the bushes and started squeezing the breath out of her. Braganza, Namdev, Mohit and Raman rushed towards the bushes without batting an eyelid. Braganza had immediately drawn his machete from the rucksack that he carried. Namdev was carrying his *kukri* in one hand and a machete in the other. Mohit had picked up a stone. They rushed beyond the bushes to see a gory sight.

The python had tightened its grip on the poor, fragile Rati. She had lost consciousness, and the creature was stretching its monstrous jaws open to devour her. Mohit threw the stone at the reptile with all the strength that he had. It was sheer luck that the stone hit it near its eye. The predator, losing its grip on Rati, now turned towards them. The other three men reached into their bags, drew out machetes and kukris, lit their torches, and charged at the python. The python sensed an imminent danger as it saw all four men rushing at it.

Braganza threw the machete at it, which struck its body, and while it was writhing in pain, the slimy reptile dropped Rati and hurriedly slid through the branches of a tree to another one and then disappeared altogether. Raman ran towards Rati and yelled, 'Rati, Rati, are you all right? Open your eyes, please.' Rati was unconscious and did not respond. Braganza felt her pulse and said, 'Thank God she is alive and safe. Let's carry her back to the trekking path and then give her first aid and some water.'

The python had not eaten anything for weeks and was damn hungry. In fact, it had not gone far, and his hunger led it back towards the path where meat for his appetite was available. It was bleeding from the injury caused by the machete, but it still kept the humans under observation. Its ambush had resulted in a misadventure, and now it was reluctant to strike at these human beings who had shown exemplary courage to make a counterattack. Any wrong move by it might get it killed.

Rati, from sheer anxiety, had developed a high fever, and Riya and Sharmila were shivering from fear. They kept looking towards the thick forest left behind. The fear in their eyes revealed their apprehensions about another attack from the rock python.

The python was also starving. Rain had started pouring down again, and the python realized that once the group moved towards Vazra Falls, it would be challenging to hunt. It was desperate and came out in the open. The person nearest to the forest was none other than Namdev, whom Braganza had sent to the rear. Before anybody could react, the giant reptile caught Namdev by wrapping its tail around his body and dragged him towards the bushes. Namdev had a horrid expression on his face and, in a second, realized that this time the reptile was better prepared and would not let go easily. The kukri had fallen from his hand, and he was helpless before the giant reptile.

The entire group was immobilized for some moments due to the ghastly act of the wretched reptile. Mike Braganza was the first one to move. He ran towards the bushes while the girls remained in the open space. Mohit and Shantanu too ran after Braganza towards the bushes. But neither Namdev nor the reptile could be seen. The reptile had moved swiftly to a dense place and could not be detected. It had no intention of leaving its meal midway.

There was pin-drop silence in the forest. There was no chirping of birds or sounds from any other animal. All had witnessed the python moving stealthily towards the open space and, after wrapping its tail around its victim, returning quickly to its hiding place, dragging the helpless Namdev with it.

The sun shone a little as the clouds parted. But the sun's rays were not of much help to the hunters who had by then become the hunted. On Mike Braganza's signal, they quickly moved towards Vazra Falls.

Disappointment was written large on their faces when all of them gathered at the open space near Vazra Falls. Though the view of Vazra Falls was breathtaking, Mike Braganza asked them to pack their rucksacks and head back to the resort.

Just then, they saw Shanta Apte, an employee of the resort, running towards them. He shouted and signalled for them to move towards Vazra Falls, saying, 'Sir, all hell has broken loose at the resort.' He took a deep breath and continued, 'Someone has torn apart the nets. The predators, leopards, pythons, wolves and reptiles have entered the resort area and are inside the precinct. Three employees are missing, and management has summoned a dozen armed rangers from the Forest Department. Some snake-catchers have also been called since some people saw a few cobras as well. It would be next to impossible to go back to the resort. It is almost as if the wild animals and reptiles have taken over the resort.' Shanta said, his voice quivering in fear, 'Sir, the wild animals have even ransacked the kitchen and the dining hall. Only with the intervention of the rangers will some normalcy be restored. When the security guards fired at the leopards and hyenas, some had already started running in this direction. Not only the guards, but the animals have also already started running in this direction. You know, sir, injured wolves and leopards are more dangerous! Please do not waste any time, run! Please run,' he pleaded, folding his hands.

Mike Braganza said, 'Are you sure? This kind of mishap has not occurred in the past three years. Damn it! We will have to take a detour and walk at least six miles to reach Ponda after crossing Vazra Falls. God, how can that kind of attack by wild animals be possible? The entire resort has always been a safe area.'

'Sir,' replied Shanta Apte, 'Vicky Sir had called the experts from Panaji to cordon off the entire resort, while I have been sent here by our manager to warn you and the guests. I heard Vicky Sir say that the net had been deliberately cut with a sharp weapon. Ironically, it is indeed an artificial, man-made error, by someone who may be on the competitor's side or someone who wanted to tarnish the resort's goodwill and image. Sir, but we do not have any time to waste. Run and save yourself, please. Many people at the resort have died.'

Mohit intervened, 'With so many deaths, it is quite obvious that someone has purposely cut the nets during the early hours of the morning, which then allowed the animals to enter the enclosed area. The entire investment of Vicky Sir will go down the drain. Today is Friday, the thirteenth. This date will come out to be unlucky for him this time.'

Braganza replied, 'I think we should leave the investigation to the Rangers and, without wasting time, move towards Vazra Falls and then turn towards Ponda village. God save the womenfolk working in the kitchen and housekeeping department of the resort. Let's move towards the waterfalls and try to save ourselves.'

All of them started to walk as fast as they could towards Vazra Falls. They had realized that, by now, certain sinister things would have happened at the resort and the wild beasts would have tasted blood. Even though wild beasts are usually afraid of humans, something changes when animals taste human blood. They often turn into man-eaters.

It was plain and simple. It was purely a case of sabotage. The nets had been intentionally cut with a machete, allowing the wild animals to enter the otherwise well-protected, peaceful, safe place.

All of them heard a shriek and looked back. A leopard was on Shanta Apte, sinking its teeth into the neck of the now lifeless body. Blood was oozing out. Mike Braganza, holding his machete, turned towards the attacker. He swirled his machete as if warning them not to come near. Just then, a pack of wolves came out into the open field.

One look at the ferocious wolves, the two leopards ran towards the dense forest and disappeared. While the two wolves stood guard around Shanta Apte's body, the others started to run in the direction of the trekkers. It was a scary sight. A pack of wolves was running after the trekkers, aiming to kill them.

Mike Braganza shouted, 'We can't kill them. They are too many in numbers. The only way out is to run towards the waterfall and jump into the river. Hope you all know how to swim. That is our only chance of survival. Let's run as fast as we can.' Rati shouted, 'We all know how to swim, except for Sharmila.' Shantanu, while running towards Vazra Falls, yelled back, 'Do not worry, I will hold her and won't let her drown. I am responsible for her safety; she is my wife.'

All of them reached the cliff, from which Vazra Falls further fell about twenty metres into the river and eventually merged with Mandovi River. The charging wolves were just a few feet away when they jumped down from the edge of the cliff. It was a big jump that anyone would hesitate to make, but it was a question of life and death.

The trekkers had the will to survive. They were also lucky since the river was deep for them to jump into without causing any injury. The moment Sharmila surfaced, Mohit and Shantanu held her. Later, Shantanu held her by the arm and swam further using the other arm. The current was strong, and they were drifting forward. Mohit looked up to find the wolves staring at them. Their eyes and mouths were blood red. Blood could be seen oozing out.

They swam for a while with the current. Alex suddenly noticed that Suzy was missing. Mike Braganza shouted, 'Alex, do not worry, the current of the river will bring her.' Just then, Suzy appeared, and Alex was relieved to see her emerging from the river bend. All of them were exhausted from swimming and wanted to swim towards the shore. Sharmila was behind, clinging to Shantanu. Out of the twelve, Suzy, a bad swimmer, was the last one.

Mandovi River was now flowing from the eastern part of Goa towards the North. The swimmers, led by Braganza, decided to swim towards the shore. Mike Braganza turned towards the shore when he noticed some fishermen on the right bank of the river. The trekkers did not see that two alligators on the other side of the shore had stealthily entered the water. They had sensed the easy prey the swimmers would make in the area they ruled. Raman noticed the second alligator as it submerged and disappeared beneath the surface. He shouted for help, and the fishermen immediately understood the reason for his panicked calls. They turned their boats towards the trekkers, who had by now lost the strength and the will to fight any other predator. They badly needed help and support.

While the alligators were approaching the trekkers fast, one of the motorboats reached the swimmers and helped a few of them aboard. Only three were left in the water when the first alligator came near them. It used its sharp teeth and tried to pull Suzy deep down into the water. Alex and Mike tried to pull her out of the grip of the beast. They struck the alligator. The alligator did, in fact, let go of Suzy, and Alex pulled her up. However, Suzy was bleeding from the alligator's bite.

The other alligator sunk its teeth into Sharmila's thigh and tried to pull her down into the deep water. Sharmila looked helplessly at her husband. Just then, Mike Braganza, holding his machete, turned towards her and hit the alligator with all his strength.

Mike swirled his machete again at the alligator. This time, the blade hit the outstretched neck of the alligator, and it immediately let go bleeding Sharmila. Another fisherman jumped into the river and quickly helped Sharmila climb onto the boat. Suzy and Sharmila were saved from becoming victims of the two alligators. But they needed medical attention as they were severely injured. Both of them had lost a lot of blood, and Suzy was also shivering. Alex was trying to tie a piece of cloth around the wound on his partner's foot. His partner had to be saved.

All of them were now onboard the two motorboats. The two injured were given first aid on the boat. The remaining trekkers were shell-shocked and could not utter a word. Sharmila had lost a lot of blood, and she fainted. Suzy was shivering from fear, and Alex continued to console her.

The moment they reached the shore the fisherman rushed the two injured women to the civil hospital at Ponda. The doctors attended to them in the emergency ward and provided the necessary medical help.

The doctors summoned the police, as was mandatory. Inspector Satish Shenai reached the spot within a few minutes. He had been informed about the incident. The fisherman, Joseph, told the inspector about the entire incident and that they had almost lost two of them to the alligators. Inspector Satish Shenai, instead of sympathizing with the trekkers, asked, 'Who amongst you is Mohit Chaddha?' Mohit came forward and said, 'Yes, sir, I am Mohit, an engineer from Bangalore. What's the matter?'

'You are under arrest for sabotage,' he asserted. 'We have reports and evidence indicating that you were responsible for the mayhem and chaos at Wild Beast Resort. You were the one who cut all the safety nets, which led the wild beasts to enter Wild Beast Resort.'

Ashu, Raman, Rati, Shantanu, and others were shocked to hear the insinuation. Mohit showed his irritation, 'What do you mean? What do I have to do with any sabotage? Sir, do you have any evidence against me? We have somehow survived the ordeal. Our lives were very much in danger. Instead of helping me, you are accusing me of sabotage. Are you crazy?'

The inspectors replied. 'There is CCTV footage from cameras placed at various strategic points inside the resort. You were seen on CCTV footage cutting the nets with Namdev's machete. You probably lifted it from his room in the early hours of the morning, cut the ropes and nets and returned it to its place. You think you are smart, eh! How much did you get from Lucky Resorts, the arch enemy and competitor of Mr Vikram sir? When did he approach you, and how much money did he offer you? You were seen in the wee hours of the morning, moving around with a machete in hand.'

Mohit calmed down a little, smiled, and replied, 'I am sure you are mistaken, sir. There is obviously some huge misunderstanding on your part. In fact, I did get up early, somewhere around 4:30 a.m., and went for a walk. I do not even know where Namdev lives within the resort. Can you please show me that footage? The allegation levelled against me is false and baseless. What would I gain from sabotaging and risking the lives of people in the resort? I would never do such a thing, not even in my dreams, sir.'

The inspector retorted sternly, 'Well, I certainly noticed you holding a machete and moving around the resort at around 4:45 a.m. What were you doing at that hour with a machete in hand?' Mohit replied, 'There was very dim light on the pathway, I was holding the machete for my own safety. I think you may have jumped the gun. I have nothing to do with any sabotage.' The inspector intervened, 'You must come with me to the police station, and I will show the footage to you. The evidence is squarely against you, Mr Mohit. You will be charged under Section 302 of the India Penal Code for the deaths of the innocent workers. Till now, four people have been killed by the rampaging beasts, and two more died in the forest, all because of your misdeed. It was a heinous crime to conspire with Lucky Resorts and carry out sabotage.'

They went to the police station at Ponda. Inspector Satish Shenai showed CCTV footage of Mohit wandering with something in his hand, but there was no footage of him using a machete to cut ropes and nets. While watching the CCTV footage, Shantanu observed that, when enlarged to a particular degree, another figure could be seen behind Mohit. The inspector had not bothered about it earlier. When the scene was enlarged at Shantanu's behest, the figure turned out to be none other than Namdev.

Mohit was stumped. 'Sir, it was Namdev himself who had given his machete to me last night. He had come to my cottage, and as I was admiring his machete, he gifted it to me, saying that he had a replica of the same.'

Sub-Inspector Pathak exclaimed, 'Sir, it was not Mohit but Namdev who did this. He was always cribbing about the meagre salary Vicky Sir gave him. Recently, he had bought a car, which he could barely afford. If we conduct a proper investigation on him, we will surely get some startling information about the sudden increase in his wealth.' Mohit stated, 'However, you will have to search for him in the forest, since a rock python has ambushed Namdev and taken him inside the dense forest.'

Inspector Satish Shenai stared at Mike. 'Oh my god, it means Namdev has already paid for his misdeeds by becoming a victim of the rock python.' Shantanu intervened, 'First, you arrest Mohit without seeing the footage properly, and then you declare Namdev to be the culprit. Please conduct your investigations properly before charging anyone with such heinous crimes.' He emphasized the last two words the inspector had used earlier.

The Inspector watched the footage again and again, and realized that Namdev was indeed the real culprit. He discharged Mohit with all the respect that he deserved for being dragged into a sabotage case that he was not involved in.

The news of the trekkers who had survived the wild beasts around Vazra Falls and the alligators in Mandovi River spread like wildfire. Many people had gathered outside the police station. As the trekkers emerged, led by Mike Braganza, the crowd began clapping joyously. The next morning, the incident was splashed all over *Navbharat Times* and other papers in Goa.

Later, the investigation revealed that Namdev had been paid five lakh rupees by a competitor to sabotage the resort's security system and give it a bad name. Vikram filed a suit against Lucky Resorts, and the police continued their investigation.

Sharmila and Suzy were later admitted to Manipal Hospital at Dona Paula, Panjim, where they recuperated and were discharged within a week. The others were lodged at Hotel Cided-De Goa, which was just opposite Manipal Hospital; the expenses of their stay were borne by Vikram, the owner of Wild Beast Resort.

The four couples heaved a sigh of relief when they boarded the flight to Bangalore. They yearned to return to the comfort of Purvan Kara, where they felt most at home and safe. Mohit commented, 'There is no doubt that trekking is adventurous, but it sure is dangerous. A mountain may welcome or deny us, but the mountains of Vazra Valley seem to have rejected us. Mercifully, all of us are aboard and returning in one piece, thanks to the massive Vazra Falls.'

BABLOO

The members of the prestigious Elite Lahore Club had some or the other connection with Lahore, now part of Pakistan but once a sought-after city of undivided India. Rita had an immense liking for Lahore, which was known for fashion and the latest designs in the pre-Partition days. Most of those present were from the Punjabi community, who had made it big in the post-independence era. They were in their mid-seventies or early eighties and had spent some time in Lahore during the pre-Partition days. Sardar Inderjeet Singh, who was a toddler when his parents shifted from Lahore to Delhi, was the only person to be the odd one out. But his parents and grandparents had lived in Lahore before Partition.

Shahid, based in Sundar Nagar, Lutyens Delhi, also hailed from Lahore. He raised a toast and said, 'Rita, I think the phrase is in a different context. A person has not taken birth if he has not seen Lahore.' Shabana, his elegant wife, intervened and said, 'Dear husband, you are right. The delicacies displayed at Anarkali Bazar, the *dobu kulcha*s of Hira Mandi and the *gulab jamun*s of Gwal Mandi are still fresh in my taste buds. I was pretty young at that time, but the days spent in Lahore were the days spent in heaven. Punjabi culture was such that, even if they were Hindu or Muslim, they were useful to each other and jointly resisted the British rule and their brutalities.

'That's true, temples and mosques co-existed, and there was harmony among the people. Punjabis wanted to progress in business. There wasn't a dull moment or depression in and around Lahore till Partition took place when the bonhomie ended in one of the worst tragedies on this planet. The bonhomie did end in one of the worst tragedies on this planet,' Rita reminisced. 'God, it was really the worst thing the Britishers could do, dividing India into three parts virtually: West Pakistan, East Pakistan and India,' Shabana complained, criticizing the British.

'You can't be far from the truth. As far as I remember, it was 14 August 1947 when Pakistan was celebrating independence,' Shahid stated as a matter of fact. 'They had to bear insults and embarrassment from their relatives for leaving Pakistan in favour of India. The sentiment was such.' A pall of gloom had descended over him while taking the train from Lahore Junction to Karachi harbour; this journey which was to be the last one from the city and its inhabitants that he had fallen in love with.

Inderjit Singh, fifty-three, a tall, burly Sikh with sharp features, butted in, 'Yes, I fully endorse your views, *chacha ji*, although I was born in Lahore in 1946, and I was an infant when I was brought to Delhi. My paternal grandparents used to live near Anarkali Bazar on Raja Ram Street. They would often go to the hill station of Murree for holidays. Everyone, be it Hindus, Sikhs, or Muslims, lived in harmony. I was told that our neighbour, Khan Chacha, would come over to our house and enter our kitchen, asking my mother to pass on some *balushahi*s to him. That was the kind of bonding they all shared. How I wish the Partition had never taken place.'

He continued after a pause, 'Millions were displaced, and thousands were killed. I have old, ancient photograph of my mother holding me in her arms at Lahore Junction when she left for Delhi in June 1947. There is a hoarding just behind my parents. On it, on a white background, "Lahore" is written in black in Hindi, English, Gurmukhi and Urdu. I have grown up listening to their praises of the inhabitants of Lahore and the musical nights with B.R. Chopra, Ramanand Sagar and Mohd Rafi at Edward Park.'

Shabana couldn't remain quiet given the topic being discussed, 'Yes, Inderjit, I remember vividly, your mother holding you in her arms at Lahore Junction whilst boarding the train to Attari, sometime in the latter part of June 1947. Your mother was my classmate and a very good friend. I had gone to bid farewell to her at the railway station. You are the youngest member of our Elite Lahore Club, aka ELC. The stalwart, Pran Nevile, who later became the Indian Ambassador to the USA, couldn't attend this get-together as he is in Luxembourg with his friend Amar Nath Sehgal's son. I remember your grandfather as a very pious man. He always wore a white turban and a long coat.' A tear welled in her eyes as she remembered Inderjit's parents and grandfather. She had indeed spent a lot of time with them in Lahore as in New Delhi.

Om Prakash Kapoor, a businessman of repute, was yet another fan of Lahore. He too intervened in the discussion and said, 'That reminds me of an amusing incident. Sometime in the 1940s, Ashok Kumar, Devika Rani and Kundan Lal Sehgal had come to Lahore by train for a film premiere. Incidentally, Congress leaders such as Nehru, Abdul Gaffar Khan and Gokhale were travelling in the same train. There was a huge crowd at the railway station to welcome the Congress leaders. Whilst garlanding Nehru, someone shouted, "Look, even Ashok Kumar, Moti Lal, Dr Sehgal and Devika Rani are alighting from the train." The entire crowd forgot about the Congress stalwarts and ran towards the film stars. Nehru was left stranded and felt humiliated. But such was the attraction and magic of film personalities.' Shabana said, 'Yes, you are right. And as far as delicacies go, Anarkali Bazar had temptations which few could resist. The Bazar had an atmosphere of fun, gaiety, laughter, vivaciousness, stretching from outside Lohari Gate to Neela Gumbad, a distance of nearly one and a half kilometres. Anarkali Bazar dominated a large part of the cityscape.'

Her husband, Shahid, sitting close by, seconded her comments, 'Yes, Kinari Bazar, Hatta, Kaseri Bazar of utensil makers, Dabbi Bazar of wholesale merchants, formed an intrinsic part of Lahore's life.'

'Yes, true,' lamented Shahid, 'Dhani Ram Bhalla was the owner of Bhalla Shoe Co., who also had to face sarcastic comments for entering the shoe business, hitherto the arena of Muslims only. Kedar Nath & Sons was another shopping Paradise.'

Shabana said, 'I do remember the huge cannon of Ahmed Shah Abdali, known as Zamzama, used by him in the Battle of Panipat in 1761. It was close to Janaki Dass & Co., Imperial

Bank and Devichands' Shop. Was it Hitkari Cycles or Hilkari Potteries?' She questioned the elder statesman.

Kapoor replied, 'Shabana, Sewa Ram Kapoor and his sons Ved and Krishan Kapoor had started the pottery business in India after Partition. They had a shop on Mall Road selling imported cycles.' Shahid smiled and said, 'Om, there was a famous hairdresser by the name of A.N. John. He was not a Britisher, but his real name was Amar Nath.'

Rita commented, 'Folks, this is January 1999, and even after three wars with Pakistan, both countries want to patch up and improve relations. Our prime minister has taken a great initiative and expressed a desire to visit Pakistan. Nawaz Sharif, the prime minister of Pakistan, has been equally receptive in inviting Shri Atal Bihari Vajpayee over to Lahore.' Inderjit questioned, 'Can we trust them. After all, they have openly announced that they want to bleed India with a thousand cuts. Look what happened in Kashmir. It was a genocide which led to an exodus of five lakh Pandits from Kashmir to the Plains.'

Om Prakash Kapoor replied, 'Inderjit, time is still the best answer. Forgiveness is still the best painkiller, and God is still the best healer. The timeless in you is aware of life's timelessness. Yesterday is today's memory and tomorrow is today's dream.'

The guests who had been talking about the Partition had now touched upon the sensitive topic of Kashmir. Rita Mehra, sensing their mood, tried to divert attention towards the lavish spread before them. She invited them to the dining table, which had multi-cuisine delicacies.

It was midnight and the discussions were still on. Inderjit

Singh bid farewell to all the members of the ELC and left the sprawling house. It was a chilling winter in January 1999, with fog enveloping the entire atmosphere. He left the host's Prithvi Raj Road residence in his chauffeur-driven car. His age-old driver, Ram Lal, while driving him down to the house, requested Inderjit to let him get down near his two-room quarter at R.K. Puram. Inderjit agreed, and on reaching R.K. Puram, he took the wheel himself. He had always been a teetotaller and was cautious while driving back home during late hours. Discussion about Partition still brought back bitter memories. The havoc and hatred it had brought had displaced many people. Inderjit was deep in thought while driving, which was a tad difficult due to the heavy fog, when the accident happened. An older woman suddenly appeared in the middle of the road.

Oblivious to the car, she tried to cross the road and in spite of Inderjit trying to brake, she got hit by the car. Inderjit had noticed her just in the nick of time and had swung the steering wheel to the right, but somehow, he had failed to stop the car in time.

The impact of the collision was such that the frail woman went up in the air for a somersault and then landed on the ground, sustaining grievous injuries. The crash was loud enough for some people to come out of the adjacent *jhuggi* cluster. Two youngsters came to his support and requested him to rush her to a nearby hospital lest she breathe her last. They gently lifted her and laid the poor, injured woman in the backseat of his car. Without bothering about the police and the aftermath, Inderjit took the wounded woman to the hospital, while constantly mumbling to himself, 'What have

I done! What have I done!' He straightaway took her to the emergency ward, where the junior doctors on duty rushed to provide medical aid to the poor woman.

The doctors, on realizing the severity of her injuries, immediately rushed the older woman towards the operating theatre. The hospital authorities had also informed the police about the accident. In a short while, the police turned up. Sub-Inspector Rathi enquired about Inderjit. Inderjit stated, 'Sir, I was driving my car when suddenly this old woman appeared in the middle of the road, and the car collided with her. Due to heavy fog, even I did not notice her till it was too late.' Sub-Inspector Rathi instructed Inderjit to summon his lawyer or relatives, as it was a matter of grave concern and consequence. He was told by the inspector not to leave the hospital without his permission.

After two hours or so, Dr Sanjeev Malik, a senior surgeon at the hospital, came out of the operating theatre and told the police personnel present there, 'Inspector, this patient is out of danger and is going to survive the ordeal. She has a brain injury along with a fractured collarbone and another fracture in her arm. She has bruises all over. It will take her at least a month to recuperate.' Inderjit Singh was relieved on hearing that the victim would somehow survive. He offered some financial aid, but the doctor declined it. Dr Sanjeev Malik told him that the government would take care of that.

Later, Inderjit was taken to the police station, and his statement was recorded under Section 164 of the India Penal Code. A case was lodged under Section 304 of the Indian Penal Code for causing grievous injuries on account of negligence. He was kept in lock-up till 4 p.m. the next day, when his lawyers, accompanied by his elder son, posted bail.

Days passed, and Inderjit Singh got busy with his business. About a month later, he received a call from the police station that he was wanted at the hospital's general ward. The frail woman had recovered from her injuries and was in a position to give a statement. Sub-Inspector Rathi told Inderjit, 'The accident happened last month. The victim has turned out to be a beggar and a widow on top of that. She was living in J.J. Colony. Please be ready to shell out some money which she is sure to ask for from someone like you who dwells in a posh locality of Vasant Vihar.' There was no response from Inderjit. Rathi continued, 'Sir, such beggars tend to take undue advantage if they get to know that they have been hit by a rich man's car. I have made enquiries and, apart from begging at the red light at Sangam Cinema Hall, it seems she has no other source of income or any relatives who can look after her. I think I am duty-bound to caution you about these living parasites.'

Inderjit replied, 'I had offered financial help earlier and am willing to do so even now. Anyway, please tell me where exactly I have to come, and I shall be there within half an hour, and I would request you to show some respect to the old lady and not call her a parasite.' Saying so, he put the phone down.

Inderjit entered the general ward of the hospital to find Sub-Inspector Rathi questioning her. She gave an inquisitive look at the tall, good-looking, fair-complexioned Sikh, who was in his early fifties but still handsome. Inderjit, in fact, seemed to be in his late thirties, but a tinge of white beard gave him away.

Inderjit Singh waited with bated breath. He was expecting her to quote an exorbitant and obnoxious figure to settle the matter between them. After all, beggars do take advantage of such situations. He was willing to part with the three lakh rupees.

Sub-Inspector Rathi, while pointing his finger at Inderjit Singh, stated, 'He was the one who was driving the car that hit you. Are you still having some concussions? Or will you be able to give your statement with respect to the hit-and-run case?'

Inderjit intervened, 'Sir, it was not a hit-and-run case. I brought her here to AIIMS hospital and am also going to take responsibility for whatever transpired that night.' Rathi grinned, revealing his crooked, tobacco-stained teeth and said, 'Sir, I have been questioning her, and she is trying to portray herself as if she is some sophisticated woman. As if I do not know these wretched beggars and their twisted intentions. Inderjit immediately cut him short, 'Inspector *sahib*, please show some respect towards her, she is old enough to be our mother.' Rathi scoffed, 'Sir, do you not know anything about these uncouth, unscrupulous beggars. They are as good as street dogs.' The beggar looked at the inspector with disgust and said, 'Inspector sahib, I know you demean us, but I have no complaints against the Sikh gentleman. With due respect, sir, he is not to be blamed for what happened that night.' Rathi looked surprised. 'Oh! Is that so? You have lost an opportunity to extract a good amount of money from him.' He then turned to Inderjit and said, 'Mr Inderjit Singh, you are lucky, sir. As far as you are concerned, the case is closed. She has emphatically withdrawn any charges against you.'

He was aware that Inderjit had not appreciated his outburst against the poor woman. He once again provoked her, 'Are you sure you want to drop charges against him and demand no compensation?'

She replied, 'Sir, to tell you the truth, it was entirely my fault. I assumed the road would be empty of vehicles at that hour.' Sub-Inspector Rathi replied, 'Look here, and listen to what I have to say. He is a rich man and lives in Vasant Vihar in a big bungalow. He has no issues with parting with some funds. Do you understand what I have just said? The rest is up to you. If you still claim, as you have in your statement, that the driver was not at fault, we have to drop the proceedings against Mr Inderjit Singh Mander. Are you sure he was not at fault? This is the last time I am asking you.'

The old woman suddenly turned towards Inderjit and said, 'Are you from Village Mander near Amritsar, Punjab?"

Inderjit replied affirmatively, 'Yes, not me, but my forefathers were indeed from Mander village in Amritsar district. That was a long time back. We are originally from Mander, madam, but why did you ask this question?' he enquired.

She replied, 'Oh, nothing, I just knew somebody from Mander village, but that was a long, long time back.' She turned to Rathi and continued, 'Sir, I am responsible for the mishap, and I am sorry for the trouble I have given to Sardarji. I am a poor woman, but I do not wish to harass someone who was not at fault. On that foggy night, the vehicle and the streetlamps on the road were out, and without looking, I ran mindlessly across the road. I am solely to blame for the accident.'

Sub-Inspector Rathi shrugged and said, 'Well, well, that settles it, sir; the case against you will be dropped after I seek approval from my seniors for the same. But I must admit she is the first one of the lot to not have pressed any charges or claimed any compensation.'

Inderjit replied, 'Please, please, please, do not use such language against her. She is my mother's age.' Inderjit Singh Mander then bowed a little before the older woman. He wanted to say something but changed his mind and left. He went towards the parking area, sat in his car and his chauffeur drove him towards the exit. Inderjit was perplexed by the old lady's mention of Mander and the fact that she had known someone of the same caste further intrigued him.

Inderjit suddenly decided that he would find out the name of the person from Mander village the old lady had been acquainted with. He stepped out of the car, asked his chauffeur to wait for some more time at the parking lot and walked towards the general ward to meet the beggarwoman once again.

Inderjit Singh raised his voice, 'Ahem! Madam, I came back to meet you out of sheer curiosity.' He waited for her to open her eyes and then said, 'I wanted to know the name of the person you were acquainted with whose surname was also Mander, and I am sorry that I have not enquired about your name. I must also admit that I am carrying three lakh rupees and intend wholeheartedly to give it to you even though you have withdrawn all charges against me.'

She shifted a little and tried to sit up on the bed, 'Why do you wish to know my name. These days, no one is bothered about the name of a beggar. I have never been to the village of Mander. I was born in Lahore and married Sohan Seth, whose father was a partner in the construction business with Sardar Ujjal Singh Mander ji. The family of Sardar Ujjal Singh ji had, in fact, come to Lahore from Mander village. They were our neighbours, and we got to know them well. I am a victim of Partition. My father had a shop at Dabi Baazar, while my father-in-law had a construction business along with Sardar Ujjal Singh ji. I am Rani, and we belonged to a well-to-do family before the Partition of India changed my life for the worse. We, in fact, lost everything in Lahore. From a rich heritage that we nurtured, we became poor after the Partition.'

She continued her saga, 'My husband was friendly with the hardworking and good-looking son of Sardar Ujjal Singh ji. His name was Amar Pal Singh Mander. Both of them were very friendly and often ate together.' Tears trickled down her face. Inderjit raised his voice and stated with excitement, '*Beeji*! Oh! Rani beeji, *waheguru*, help me! You, you… I have found you at last. You are Mrs Rani Seth; oh, I can't believe my luck. I am Inderjit, Amar Pal Singh Mander's son.' This time, tears appeared in the eyes of Inderjit Singh. He wiped his tears and continued, 'Oh! What a coincidence. The names you have just taken are no one else's but my father's and my grandfather's. My father was indeed a partner and a very close friend of your husband, Mr Sohan Seth. You would not know, but whenever he reminisced about the days spent in Lahore, he would always mention you and your husband's names and talk endlessly about the good times he had spent with your family there. I am blessed to have come in contact with you. I know everything about you, beeji. Oh! Can I call you beeji?'

Rani was astonished. This was bizarre. She took a deep breath and then enquired in her feeble voice, 'Is...is your father, Amarpal Singh ji, alive? And your mother? Is she alive? Can I meet them? It's been so long, how are they?'

'No, beeji, they passed away some time back. I wish they were alive. Nevertheless, they always talked about your family.' Inderjit paused for a while and then said, 'I am not going to let my beeji live in a J.J. Cluster or here at a government hospital. I am going to get you discharged from this hospital and get you admitted to the best private hospital in Delhi. I think I am duty-bound to do that.'

Rani protested, 'No, Inder, I am fine. I hardly have much time left… I am a patient of asthma and would not like to trouble you with my plight and my miseries. No, no, Inder, there is no need. I will continue to live in the cluster. I do not wish to disturb you or your family.' But Inderjit Singh, the gentleman that he was, insisted that she allow him to help her recover quickly. He was adamant and wanted make all the arrangements for shifting her to a private hospital in South Delhi, from where he wanted take her to his house in Vasant Vihar. He told her, 'Beeji, please do not take away the chance to look after my second mother. Beeji, there is a reason why I am calling you my second mother. You might have forgotten, but I haven't. When I was born, I was told that my mother was anaemic. There was no blood bank at the Civil Hospital in Lahore. The doctors told my father that they could either save the mother or the child. My mother had told me that you were the one who gave her blood that was urgently needed. That saved my mother and me. Beeji, how can I forget that? I am negative O, and so are you. Beeji, please do not refuse my offer. I owe it all to you and you only. The mother and the newborn could survive only because of the blood you donated. Your blood runs in my veins, Beeji. You are my godmother.'

While preparations were being made to discharge her from the hospital, Inderjit held her hands and sat down next to her. He asked her about her deplorable condition and the reasons for it.

Rani Seth went down memory lane to tell him by what quirk of fate she had become a poor beggar. She narrated, 'It was the month of August 1947 when India and Pakistan were being partitioned. My father-in-law had decided to continue to live in Lahore as minorities. That turned out to be a bad decision. On 11 August 1947, a mob had planned to descend upon our bungalow with *mashal*s (fire torches), knives and swords to put an end to our lives and snatch whatever we possessed. Javed, who was a twenty-one-year-old close friend of my husband, had come to our aid. He came to know from his servant about the gruesome plan of killing the Hindus staying at No. 5, Raja Ram Street. Without wasting even a moment he rushed to our house to inform us about the imminent danger that we were in. But my father-in-law would not listen to him. He was adamant and had an argument with Javed and was not inclined to leave Lahore at any cost. He had even taken out his three knot rifle to defend us.

I had heard Javed pleading with him vociferously. I clearly remember his words. He had said, 'Chacha ji, a mob has gathered outside the house of Rehmat Ali, and they are all planning an assault on your family. Believe me, you shall not be able to save yourself. Please run towards the railway station from the back door, and all of you save your lives. Time is of the essence. Leave everything as it is. Just run for your life, and save yourself and your family. Please, please, chacha ji, listen to me for god's sake. Run away to safety while you can.' Inderjit stated, 'That was very nice on his part to warn you, even at a big risk to himself.' 'Yes, Inder, you are right, Javed turned out to be our saviour,' she agreed with him.

She continued her tale, 'The fanatics had decided not to allow any Hindu to stay on this side of the border. The primary reason was that almost all the Hindus were richer than the Muslims, and that was the easiest way to usurp their properties and wealth. Greed and revenge had overpowered their sensibilities and ethics. A day before, the train had arrived from Amritsar full of corpses, now the fanatics were heading towards Seth Mahal to ransack and kill us. There was an acute sense of urgency in the voice of Javed. Rani, while telling her saga, started to weep. Inderjit held her hand and offered her a glass of water. She drank a few sips and then continued her story.

'Sohan, my husband, had stood scandalized for some moments whilst I had yelled at Javed, "What are you saying, Javed bhai? Jinnah has just announced that the Hindus who wish to stay in the newly formed Pakistan can do so." But he kept saying, "It is too dangerous for you to stay any longer. Please leave, and once the riots and these mindless assaults have subsided, you can come back to your house. But for now, please leave for Attari by the first train that you can catch. Forget about everything else, save yourself." He continued to plead vehemently.' She paused a little, drank some water and then continued, 'Sohan, who had not moved an inch, asked him in a hushed tone where Attari was and what would become of my parents and also the jewellery and money that was there in the house. "What will happen to my investment in Ujjal Singh and Sons, and what about the pending railway contracts the Britishers have given us? They should save us from the fanatics," he obstinately kept saying. He then turned to face me and asked, "What will happen to your shop, Kailash Nath and Sons, and your parents? Rani what are we supposed to do? Will the British save us from these fanatics?"

'Javed then shouted once again, "Oh! Sohan! Why are you being so naive? Is your life more important than your wealth? Please leave with Bauji, Amma, Rani Bhabhi and your infant son. Things have gone from bad to worse. Run, run, and save your lives."

'I ran towards my son, who was in the arms of my father-in-law. We decided to leave through the back door. My father-in-law was somehow still concerned about the money and jewellery that were stashed in the vault affixed to a wall in the inner room of Seth Mahal. He handed the infant to me and told the three of us to dash towards the railway station. I remember his last words,' she said and again paused while wiping the tears on her cheeks with her fingers.

'We waited for my father-in-law at the corner of the back street. When he did not turn up, my husband rushed back to find that he had changed his mind and instead of throwing the valuables in the well, he had started digging a pit with a sickle near the banyan tree. My husband came rushing, and from the back street we ran through the by-lane towards the railway station. He had decided to bury the valuables, and only then would he leave for the station. We heard gunfire and realized that he was the one who had fired at the mob with his .303 rifle. We continued to run towards the station, hoping against hope for him to catch up with us.'

Inderjit was curious about the family's fate. He asked, 'Were all of you able to cross the border?' She replied, 'That was not to be; there was a big fanatic mob at the station, and without waiting for my father-in-law, we jumped on a moving train which was leaving for Wagah Border. In the melee, someone pushed me and I lost control of my dearest and only child. He fell down from the running train on the platform and on being hurt started crying aloud. I thought of pulling the chain, but then saw my mother-in-law picking up my son and holding him in her arms. My husband, too, was desperate to either jump from the train or pull the chain. But the crowd was in such a frenzy and panic that it was impossible. Within minutes, the train had left Lahore Junction and was heading towards the border. Both of us were desperate but there was no respite. The only hope was my mother-in-law somehow managing to reach the refugee camp at Amritsar with my son,' she said, starting to weep once again. 'After all, the distance was hardly thirty to forty miles,' she explained.

Inderjit enquired, 'Beeji, you mean Bauji, Amma and your son were left in Lahore only. You mean to say they never reached Amritsar? Waheguru! Waheguru! What happened to them?'

'Inder, that was the last time I saw my mother-in-law or my son. Later on, when we made inquiries through the police at the refugee camp, we came to know that there were dead bodies lying scattered all over the city of Lahore. The police had performed the last rites of the dead *en masse*. As per police reports my in-laws and my only son had died on 11 August 1947. I should have jumped down or pulled the chain, but that was not possible. The frenzied mob killed my mother-in-law and my seven-month-old child at the station itself. My father-in-law died at the house while defending himself.' Tears trickled down her cheeks in abundance as she narrated her ordeal. Inderjit maintained silence and after a few minutes said, 'Beeji why didn't you contact us? We would have taken care of you and Sohan Uncle.'

She looked at Inderjit and said, 'Do you know that Sardar Ujjal Singh ji, your grandfather, had a brother by the name of Sardar Santokh Singh. When your great-grandfather passed away, your great-grandmother, Karamjit Kaur, called her two sons to divide the properties among the two brothers. Without even a single word or any argument they amicably agreed to divide the properties in Lahore and Delhi between themselves. While your grandfather lost everything in Lahore, Rawalpindi and Sialkot and became a penniless refugee, his real brother gained a fortune in independent India. That is what is called destiny. I know this because I met them at the refugee camp in Amritsar. I do not know what happened thereafter. With a tryst of destiny, India gained independence but your grandfather lost all his properties on that side of the border. At the refugee camp, he and your parents were in a sorry state of affairs. So, on what basis could we have asked your parents to help us?'

Inder consoled her and said, 'Beeji, many untoward things happened during that time. Millions, on both sides of the border, were displaced. Many went to Pakistan and millions came to India. My grandfather and other members lived with

Sardar Santokh Singh ji who also helped my grandfather to re-establish himself in independent India. It took a long time but we established ourselves and eventually succeeded. Please, beeji, come with me. I beg of you. Treat me like your son. After all, your blood runs in my veins.' Rani reluctantly agreed. Inder took her to a private hospital for further treatment. In about a week, she was discharged. He brought her home and gave her a well-furnished bedroom and all other material comforts. His wife and two sons welcomed her with open arms.

Rani Seth had finally got what she had deserved a long time back. One day she told her newfound son, 'Inderjit, can you fulfil a desire that I have cherished for a long time. I have lived this long, only in the hope of fulfilling one wish. I have seen on television that our prime minister, Atal Behari Vajpayee ji, is planning a trip to Lahore to meet Pakistan's prime minister, Nawaz Sharif. I want to visit Lahore for the last time. It has been fifty-two years since I left that city. But I do wish to go back one last time. Can you help me to be a part of the prime minister's entourage which will leave for Lahore on 18 February 1999 for Lahore? It is a golden opportunity that I do not wish to miss out on.'

Inderjit said, 'Beeji, of course, why not! But, will you achieve anything by going all the way. A lot has changed in these fifty-two years. Neither your house nor your in-laws' house at Raja Ram Street would be in the same condition as it was in 1947. The attempt might turn out to be futile and a disappointment of sorts.'

Rani took a deep breath and said, 'I want to go to Lahore. I want to visit both of my houses at Mall Road and Raja Ram

Street and meet the present occupants. Even if everything has changed and they do not treat me well, I still want to see the house where I was born and the house where I spent the best time of my life after my marriage. I want to see Anarkali Bazar and the Baba Lalu Temple situated in the midst of Anarkali Bazar. I want to visit Nankana Sahib at Sheikhupura district. I was born in Lahore; my roots belong there.'

Inderjit Singh replied, 'Beeji, it's been years since the Partition took place and that is a thing of the past. You will find a sea change in Lahore, and it won't be worthwhile for you to visit Pakistan, especially in this medical condition. But if you really want to go, I have some good contacts and I think I can fulfil this desire of yours. I can surely obtain a visa for you, beeji. If you wish, I can come along with you.' She replied, 'Inder, please let me go back on my own. I have troubled you a lot, but please let me go. I want to visit Lahore before I die.'

Inderjit made all the necessary arrangements and Rani Seth, after a gap of fifty-two years, was en route to Lahore, aboard Samjhauta Express on 18 February 1999. This was a date that the country would never forget. The bus carrying the prime minister of India, Atal Bihari Vajpayee, the actor, Dev Anand, a famous lyricist, Javed Akhtar, the cricketer Kapil Dev, and others, arrived at Lahore in style. They were received by an entourage led by Prime Minister Nawaz Sharif.

There was once again a bonhomie not witnessed before between the two arch enemies. For Rani, it was a sort of homecoming. She was twenty-one years old when she had got married to Sohan Seth on 18 February 1945 at Lahore. She had tears in her eyes when she came out of Lahore

Station. She had expected a lot of changes, and she had been apprehensive that she would not be able to recognize certain places in Lahore.

Surprisingly for her, there was hardly any change which she could notice at Lahore Junction. The only change visible was the chairs and tables replacing the old worn-out wooden benches. Delhi, Mumbai and Bangalore had progressed tremendously, but Lahore still had the same look as it had in the 1940s when she had left it. The names of certain places had not been changed at all. Only the Hindi hoardings and name plates were conspicuous by their absence. Everything seemed to be in either Urdu or English.

She stood looking at the crowd, moving in tandem. She hired a taxi which took her via Lawrence Road to her hotel situated at Civil Lines. She checked in, kept her luggage and, shortly thereafter, left for her ancestral home at Mall Road, the house where she was born. To her dismay her house had been demolished and replaced by a huge store. She immediately left for Raja Ram Street and was surprised to learn from the taxi driver that the street's name was still the same. Even after fifty-two years, the narrow roads and the zamama existed.

She had not forgotten the place where the showroom of Kailash Nath and Sons at Dabi Bazaar and the 'Baba Lalu temple' in the midst of Anarkali Bazaar used to be. Her heartbeat increased when she reached 5, Raja Ram Street, just behind the *bazaar*. She got out of the taxi and had a long look at her old house. Even the red bricks of the outer wall had remained somewhat unchanged. The wooden door at the entrance had been changed to something which was more formidable than what it had been fifty-two years ago.

Reluctantly, she pressed the bell button affixed on the right side of the door and waited with an increased palpitation in her heart for someone to open the door. What if the occupant did not allow her inside? What if he misbehaved with her? What if there was no one in the house? Many such thoughts crossed her mind. 'Oh, I would have come all the way from Delhi in vain, then,' she murmured to herself.

A voice came from inside, 'Who's there?' She replied, 'Rani… Rani Seth from Delhi.' The lady of the house, who opened the door, was dressed in a white embroidered *salwar kameez*. She was almost her own age with grey hair neatly tied on one side and *kajal* (kohl) in both her eyes. She looked elegant and was someone who had a very pleasing personality and seemed to be congeniality personified.

Rani, with a lump in her throat said, 'Sister, I am Rani Seth from Delhi. A long time back, we used to live here. It was before the Partition took place. I got married in 1945 and came here to live in this house, which once belonged to my in-laws. I have come along with the Indian prime minister on a goodwill visit to Pakistan. This house at that time was known as Seth Mahal.'

Fatima Begum, the lady of the house, responded with an expression of pleasant surprise, '*Ya khuda*, you have come all the way from Delhi to your old house in Lahore. That's remarkable.' She welcomed her and yelled at her maid servant, 'Sakina, bring some sharbat for the real owner of Seth Mahal.' She gave more instructions in a tone that revealed her excitement, 'Sakina, call Kaalu and tell him to cook some good delicacies for our revered guest. Oh sorry, I mean for the real owner of this house.' Rani looked amazed as Fatima laughed loudly and clapped her hands like a schoolgirl. She was quite old but still had that girlish charm.

'Rani,' she beckoned her, 'please come in and feel as comfortable as possible. This is as much yours as it is mine. In fact, it was your house and will remain yours only. We have just been occupying it. Feel at home, dear sister.' Rani had not expected such a warm welcome from a stranger, that too in Pakistan. All her apprehensions had been put to rest by such a warm response from Fatima Begum.

In a few minutes, delicious eatables were placed before her. They chatted about their past and their respective families for a while. Time seemed to pass quickly. It was bonhomie from the minute she entered her old house. Rani was in tears, but those tears were of joy and happiness. She went to all the rooms and the terrace, and spent some time in each room, as if she was in a trance, reminiscing about the good times spent in these very rooms. Time had stopped for a while.

The setting sun prompted Rani to bid farewell, and she asked for permission to leave by saying, 'Khuda hafiz to you, Fatima Begum. I am overwhelmed by your hospitality and love. In spite of my advanced age, it was still a good decision to come all the way to Lahore.' The lady of the house who was all smiles, in turn, requested her to stay for some more time in the home where Rani had indeed entered as a bride and spent her wedding night. On her insistence, Rani stayed for a little while and was offered another cup of tea by the Pakistani occupant. She was surprised to notice that there was hardly any difference between her and Fatima's Punjabi dialect, mannerisms and food habits. Some Hindi words thrown in here and there made it look as if Fatima was a next-door neighbour from Delhi.

With some hesitation and reluctance, this time Rani asked her newfound friend if she could help her in finding the two jewellery boxes that had been left there by her father-in-law. She was in a dilemma, but on seeing Fatima's affectionate demeanour, she gathered the courage to mention her jewels.

Fatima was taken aback. She said, 'Oh! You mean the rumours were correct. Some people around here had indeed informed us that most of the Hindus had thrown their jewellery boxes into the wells located in their respective houses. My husband made our servants dive down in the well several times, but nothing could be found. Are you sure your father-in-law threw the valuables in the well?'

Shrugging her shoulders, Rani replied, 'Yes, most of them did that. They were all under the impression that they would somehow return and take care of their precious belongings. My father-in-law did not throw it in the well but had dug a pit near the banyan tree in that courtyard.' She pointed to the place where it was dug and said, 'In case it is found then half of it is yours, dear sister. I will be content with just one box in case it is found, though the chances are slim. I would not mind parting with one box.'

Fatima immediately called her faithful servant, Kaalu. She asked him to bring a sickle and dig out the boxes from the place pointed out by Rani. Fatima reassured her, 'Do not worry, this old servant, Kaalu, can be trusted. He has served us for more than forty years and is the same age as my son.'

While the servant began digging, Fatima and Rani sat nearby, breathless. After digging for some time, the sickle hit the outer rims of the two boxes. The servant took them out of the pit with abundant caution. Rani was given the boxes. She removed the dirt and opened them one by one.

Sparkling diamond jewellery with rubies and emeralds dispelled the darkness in the courtyard. The jewellery was amazing. A *rani haar* (queen's necklace) made of gold was studded with at least thirty rubies and was worth at least twenty lakhs.

Rani looked at it in amazement and exclaimed, 'Fatima ji, my husband had purchased this necklace for me on our first anniversary in 1946!' Rani was ecstatic with delight. The newfound boxes felt like a return of the riches she had lost during the Partition. She offered one half of the jewellery to Fatima Begum, who politely declined and said, 'Look, sister, I am a widow and live with my son, Fuzail. I already feel sad that you had to leave your business and precious items on this side of the border. Your parents also died in Lahore. How on Earth can I claim a share in this jewellery? It belongs to you in its entirety, and I have no right over it. We have met today only but I feel as if we were sisters in our previous birth. Please do not embarrass me any further. These boxes always belonged to you and will always remain yours.'

Rani thanked her profusely while holding the precious jewellery boxes in her lap. Fatima gave some money to her servant and told him to keep this event a secret. Rani was ecstatic at having found the jewellery. She was also flabbergasted by this newfound friendship with a fascinating person, Fatima Begum of Lahore, who had no qualms about entertaining and going out of the way for an Indian visiting Lahore after a gap of fifty-two years.

Rani once again went to the bedroom where she used to sleep with her husband and reminisced about the good times they had had there. She told Fatima, 'Dear sister, when I had entered this house as a bride, my mother-in-law had poured some oil at the doorstep to welcome me. It's considered auspicious. I still remember that day vividly. Oh my God, it seems as if all that happened just yesterday.'

Both of them laughed at the change of events. Rani was overwhelmed with joy. She said, 'Fatima ji, I will never forget this visit to my old home. If I had any grudge about the Partition, it is no longer there. I forgive those fanatics and the ones who took everything away from me.'

Fatima replied, 'Forget the past, sister, and see if you can come here more often. My husband passed away three years ago. My son, Fuzail, works as a marketing manager at Philips Pakistan, Inc., and is mostly on the road. You are most welcome to come and stay with me whenever you wish and as long as your government permits. In fact, you must stay on a little more as Fuzail is due to arrive any time. You must meet him before you head back to your hotel. I will ask him to drop you. I want to see his reaction when I tell him that the real owner of this house has come all the way from Delhi.'

Rani apologized to her and said, 'Fatima ji, I have already overstayed. Thanks a lot for your hospitality. But I must admit that only God knows that I do not wish to leave so soon. I had vowed that in case I receive my valuables, I shall pay my homage and respect at Nankana Sahib.'

Fatima Begum was not one to be rebuffed. She tightly held her hands and requested that she stay for a while, 'Fatima

Begum, thanks to you, I received the valuables, but I must tell you that the most precious was my seven-month-old son, who was killed at the railway station and how I wish someone would come and say, "Hey Rani, he is very much alive and here he is."'

Fatima intervened, saying, 'Did you make any efforts to trace him? After all, how can you be sure that he was killed? He, being a toddler, may have been left by the fanatics or may have somehow survived the ordeal.'

Rani replied, 'We tried our best to trace him. In fact, one of my uncles had been allowed to visit Lahore after five years of Partition. We had asked him to try and find something about our only child. But he came back to India empty-handed, and that was certainly a great disappointment.'

Fatima said, 'But, dear sister, how on Earth could he have traced your child after five years? Your son, if he was alive, would have changed quite a lot. Some Hindu orphans I know of were converted to our faith. But finding someone after five years is an uphill task. You had given him a difficult task.' Rani said, 'Fatima Begum, my seven-month-old son had a distinct feature. Due to that feature my uncle would have certainly recognized him if he had found him.'

Fatima Begum said, 'Tell me, dear sister, I am all ears. What distinct feature are you talking about?' Rani once again went down memory lane. 'Fatima Begum, a unique thing happened when my son was born on 25 January 1947. My maternal uncle came to meet us at the Civil Hospital in Lahore. He had held my son in his arms and announced that my son was unique and would shine in whatever field he chose. After five days when I was being discharged, he again came to the hospital. Holding my son in his arms,' he exclaimed, 'Rani, the child that I am holding in my arms is actually not your son. I thought you would have noticed. This child is definitely not your son since I had noticed that he had a hole in his left ear lobe. A big hole, something like a birthmark. I am absolutely sure I had noticed it. This child is certainly not your son. A big furore took place, then. The hospital authorities summoned the staff on a complaint from my husband. After investigation, the nurse admitted to having goofed up. My son, with a hole in the left ear lobe, was traced and found next to another lady called Lajwanti, who had given birth to a child at the same time on the same day. Because of this distinct feature which was noticed by my mama ji, I got my son back. However, that happiness lasted only for the next seven months when the cruel hands of destiny took him away from me forever.' Fatima Begum suddenly got up and embraced her tightly. Tears of happiness trickled down her cheeks. She gave a mischievous smile to Rani and said, 'You said nothing has changed in Lahore, but I think a lot has changed for you. Didn't I ask you to wait for my son to arrive?'

Rani paused, wiping her tears from her hand. There was a pin-drop silence, broken only when Fatima Begum started laughing. She was laughing rather hysterically whilst simultaneously clapping her hands. The girlish charm had surfaced again but this time her laughter had a different tenor all together.

Just then the doorbell rang and someone shouted while entering the courtyard, 'Amma, I am back. The tour was hectic. Fuzail stopped on seeing Rani sitting along with her mother. She was a stranger to him.'

Rani, lost in memories of her past, was shocked to see the good-looking, tall man walking towards her. Fatima smiled at her and said rather dramatically, 'Hey Rani, he is very much alive. Dear sister, here comes your son. You seemed shocked because he would in all probability resemble your husband. I have not seen your husband but your expression tells it all.' She waited for a response. Rani just stood like a rock. Fatima laughed and continued, 'Of course, he does not know, but I guess destiny reveals the truth one way or the other. Your only son is right in front of you in flesh and blood. Fuzail is no one else but the infant you left on the platform in your mother-in-law's arms on that fateful day.'

Rani could not control herself while Fuzail looked at his real mother in utter disbelief. He could not believe what was being uttered in front of someone who he was seeing for the first time in his life. With a bewildered expression, he said, 'Amma, amma, what are you talking about?'

Fatima begum cleared her throat and said, 'Well, on that fateful day, the infant was not killed. Someone picked him up and took him to the police station. The police later sent him to an orphanage. I could not bear a child. We went to the orphanage to adopt and they gave him to us. Since the age of three years, he has been with us, and since we had no knowledge about his date of birth, we kept the date on which we adopted him as his birthday. That date was 18 December 1950.' Rani had a lump in her throat when she said, 'Fatima Begum, 18 December is the date of birth of my husband Sohan ji. That can by no means be a coincidence.' She started to weep.

Fatima Begum, too, had tears in her eyes. She said, 'See the hole in his left earlobe? When you narrated the incident that had happened when he was born, I realized there and then that the child that we had adopted was yours and yours only. The unique feature reveals his true identity,' Fatima said this in a soft yet shaky tone.

Rani got up and hugged her long-lost son for a long, long time. With tears in her eyes, she said, 'Nothing had changed in Lahore but a tremendous change has come to my life within one day that I have spent here. First, I got my entire jewellery back and became self-reliant and then Fuzail, my son! God, I cannot digest so much happiness at the same time. Waheguru, please give me strength. Now I do not wish to die. I want to live to see my grandchildren.' Fatima asked her, 'We gave your son the name Fuzail. He remembers his father a lot.' Fatima called upon Kaalu and asked him to touch Rani's feet. She said, 'Kaalu, touch your godmother's feet. She is the one who held you in her arms and fed you with her milk for four to five days before you were given back to your mother.' Rani almost jumped and said, 'What are you saying?' Fatima replied, 'Rani, my dear sister, the orphanage from where Kaalu came, told us that he too was born to a Hindu lady known as Lajwanti, who gave birth to him on the same day, and his parents died in the aftermath of partition. The nurse who had goofed up had revealed that incident to the caretaker of the orphanage. We celebrate Kaalu and Fuzail's birthday on the same day.'

Rani could not believe her ears; neither could she believe what she had just witnessed. She embraced Fuzail once again. Fatima Bibi asked her, 'What did you use to call him after he was born on 25 January 1947, and later, for the next seven months?' Rani gulped and tried to speak, but no voice came out. Emotions were choking her voice.

Fatima Begum asked her once again, 'Dear sister, what did you call your son?' Rani paused a little, took a deep breath and then said, 'Babloo.'

TULIP COBRAS

'Rob a bank, rob a government treasury, rob a cash van, but do not ever think of robbing the sacred lake, which has probably the largest, most immense treasure of gold and diamonds in the world,' Monty said, now speaking aloud. His voice was rising at the same pace as his heartbeat. He had high blood pressure, a sugar problem and an uncanny habit of speaking aloud, a hint of anxiety audible in the high pitch. He continued, his excitement, unabated, 'There is a mythological story attached to it. Anybody who has sneaked into or around the sacred lake and robbed the treasure, or even a part of it, has been bitten by hundreds of cobras present in and around the temple. They guard the treasure lying at the bottom of the lake. So, my dear friends, forget the idea of extricating any treasure from the lake in that godforsaken holy place in Himachal.'

The five inmates had been imprisoned for life and were sentenced to be hanged till death. They were in barrack no. 4, jail no. 16, in Tihar Jail, Delhi, for the heinous crimes they had committed. After profuse appeals to the highest authorities, the apex court had finally condemned them.

They were waiting for relief on account of a mercy plea, a petition they had submitted to the president of India. All of them except for Monty had not only jointly conducted a bank heist but had also gunned down three security guards, four police personnel and the bank manager before being caught red-handed by the authorities. There were several other cases of murder, dacoity, arson and kidnapping pending in the courts against them. Each of these men had a price on his head and was among the most hardened criminals in the country.

Suleiman, trying to calm him down, said, 'Monty, you control your temper. Why do you have to get excited? Just relax, buddy, we are only discussing this fascinating story that you have pulled out like a rabbit from a hat.'

ACP Manjit Singh, a tall Sikh with a large belly, walked leisurely. The discussion was leisurely towards them with two sentries behind him, and he asked them about the hot topic of discussion and the reason for such a heated discussion, which was audible from afar.

'Nothing, sir, we were just discussing a thriller movie and its plot,' Monty replied, trying not to reveal the truth. He couldn't have, even if he had wanted to.

ACP Manjit Singh retorted, 'I hope you are not discussing *Sholay* again,' and chided them, saying, '*Hum bhi angrezon ke zamaane ke jailer hain* (Even I am a jailer from the British era).' All the inmates laughed at his mimicry of a famous comedian.

'We are celebrating the new year on the 1 January at the lawn outside Jail 14. All of you have to attend the celebration whether you like it or not,' he said with authority. 'And no excuses,' he added sternly, before again saying sarcastically, 'I have stomach trouble, sir. I have a headache, sir. Nothing doing! Is that understood?' he asked, raising his voice.

The hardened criminals remained silent. They knew they would not attend the celebrations, which was a tedious, dull affair for them. They had different plans. The jailer, however, was an experienced hat. He had sensed that. These criminals of the highest order were once again hatching a plot of some sort.

He smiled and laughed. He knew no one could dare deny him the pleasures of being sarcastic whenever he wanted, especially when he was laughing at condemned prisoners. He came closer and whispered a bit whimsically, 'No mischief and no funny business. Remember, I am the jailer here, and I rule over this place. Moreover, you good-for-nothing hoodlums, I have not received my instalment for last month. If I do not receive it as promised, I will put you in Barrack 1, where you will rot to death. I will withdraw all the facilities I have given you in these barracks. No TV, no movies on the VCR, no chicken or mutton. I want my money by this weekend, you scoundrels!' he again yelled, while casually walking towards the main door of Jail 16. 'Remember, the new year is ushering in a new millennium—2000. You are lucky that the president has not dismissed your petitions yet; otherwise, you would not have been fortunate enough to see the morning of January 2000.'

While turning by the corridor, he again raised his voice, 'No mischief, otherwise I will kill you with my bare hands before the president rejects your mercy petitions. Join in, since it is going to be a celebration worth attending. Special arrangements are being made to welcome the new millennium; we are ushering in the twenty-first century, and you should consider yourself lucky to be alive. Am I clear?'

The five condemned prisoners yelled unanimously, 'Yes, sir,' and waited for him to leave, and then all of them smiled, a sinister one.

Suleiman said, 'The jailer will faint if he comes to know that we won't be in this goddamn place on the last night of the twentieth century. The arrogant, stupid jailer thinks too much of himself. I will teach him a lesson one day.' While saying so, Suleiman clenched his fists. Suleiman was a powerfully built man who had killed the security guard with his bare hands, squeezing the air out of him.

Shaka, who scored a tad over Suleiman and was indeed the most rugged, dreaded and lethal of all of them, got up with a snarl, 'One day, I will kill this ACP, and that will stop his laughter once and for all. I will put a slug in his heart. Bullets do not know whom they are targeting.' He laughed and turned to Suleiman and asked, 'What about the consignment of drugs which is ready for delivery? You have someone to beat up someone once again so that they can be sent to the Civil Hospital? There, the doctor on our payroll will put a plaster on his hands and insert the packets in it before the plaster dries up. Hurry it up, we have hardly any time, and the demand for drugs before New Year's Eve is the highest ever. The ACP knows this but keeps quiet as long as the instalments are being paid by us.'

Shaka then turned to Monty and barked, 'I will go to the bloody holy lake, take a dip, and come out with the biggest haul ever. Monty, you have a weak heart and blood pressure issues, you remain here in your barracks. Moreover, I do not intend to wait for the president to dismiss our mercy petition and send us to the gallows. I know when a rope will be tied around my neck, this goddamn jailor would smile. I would rather die at the lake, bitten by those slimy reptiles, than see him smile.' As he said so, his scar-stretched face gave him a sinister look. He was taller than all the other four dreaded intimates and had links with the underworld dons who supplied drugs.

'Who the hell wants to be here and wait for the president to reject the mercy petition? If we do not escape, we will all be hanged anyway.' Suleiman intervened and continued his tirade against the system, 'Why not find a way while the sun shines in the tunnel, steal the treasure and vamoose to oblivion where this ACP or the authorities can't dream of reaching us ever.'

Shaka's handyman, Rakesh, was massaging his shoulders and trying his best to give him relief from a frozen shoulder. He was all muscle, and no one in the entire prison dared to mess around with him. No one dared to sit near Shaka while having lunch or dinner in the dining hall. They were all scared of him and his temper. Rakesh was short in height, almost a foot shorter than Shaka, but was burly. He was a hoodlum who behaved as Shaka's henchmen and would do as was ordered by him.

Monty did not have the heart to counter Shaka. Assessing the mood of the convicted criminal and the mobster, he immediately backed out. Another inmate, Sunder, had not spoken a word and had remained silent throughout the discussion. He, too, had killed many people in the past forty-nine years of his life. He was a hoodlum and a trained shipper who took up assassination assignments.

Shaka again spoke, 'Monty, you are condemned because you killed that police inspector while on the run from that art gallery in Naggar, Manali, or wherever. That was in self-defence, but I have never killed in self-defence. I have shot people dead or put a knife to their throats because I had all the intention of killing them. You guide us, and we will reach that place and rob the jewels and whatever money we can lay our hands on. If we failed in the bank heist, we shall not fail in stealing the temple's wealth. I personally feel that given the absence of any security around the temple, it will be an easy task. I am wondering as to why nobody has thought of making off with the jewels in the lake.'

Sunder was well-built and tall. He could not match the strength of Shaka, but he had a lot of guts. He was the quickest in drawing a gun at his opponents. He was also a confident person. But it was precisely due to his overconfidence that the four men had been caught by the police on the spot.

He finally spoke, 'I am going there with Shaka and Suleiman, whether you like it or not. Why do you believe in such silly hocus-pocus?' He tilted his shoulder awkwardly and, raising his crooked fingers, mocked Monty and said, 'The tulip flowers turn into cobra snakes, and the one who tries to steal any item from the lake becomes their victim. They are present in thousands, and no number of bullets can stop so many cobras from striking at you. During the daytime, they are tulip flowers guarding the temple but turn into cobras in the dark of night. Are you crazy, man?'

All of them laughed at his mimicry. Suleiman took it up

from there. 'It is such a joke, a tulip turning into a dangerously poisonous cobra. Monty, you must be mad to believe this kind of story. Stop being superstitious, you silly fellow,' he said, raising his voice. Monty remained silent.

Sunder butted in, 'If the locals of that area believe in such a mythological story, let them do so. These uneducated, religious, superstitious, naive Hindus deserve to be doomed, if they believe in such silly folklore. Let's steal the booty that lies on the bottom of the lake and make merry! What do you say, buddies?'

'Monty, brother, listen,' spoke Suleiman, 'It's time to steal the biggest treasure of all time. If there are some age-old idols, we will steal them too, and in doing so, if we have to kill a few priests or workers or pilgrims, we shall not budge.' He laughed again, 'After all, even if you kill one or kill many, the punishment is the same—hanged till death,' he said, emphasizing the last three words. 'And we are already condemned to hang till death by the Supreme Court,' he finished.

Monty was at his defensive best, 'Suleiman, this holy place is at a height of 12,000 feet above sea level and is situated in the remotest part of Himachal Pradesh. Everybody leaves the temple and its surroundings by dusk, and not even a soul dares to stay there at night. The priest and the workers return in the morning at around 7 a.m. to open the temple gates and perform the first set of prayers at 7.30 a.m. This routine has been followed for the past several hundred years now. Nobody has dared to stay there at night. Some foolish people did try a few times but heard strange noises and the howling of wolves. The tulip cobras and other animals have attacked many people in that area who tried to steal the treasure from the holy lake. Believe me, I was there, albeit during the daytime, and I could feel those tulip-like cobras staring at me.'

He paused for a reaction and continued, 'The pilgrims start pouring in by 9 a.m. from all adjoining and far-flung areas, and after performing their prayers, they go over to the bank of the lake and offer jewellery, copper, silver articles and money to the lake. Some of them allegedly claim that when they stayed a little longer after sunset, they saw all the purple-coloured tulips turning into poisonous cobras to guard the treasure in the temple as well as the in the lake,' Monty blurted in one breath.

'When thieves looked at the temple, nothing happened. But when they looked at the lake and its treasure and tried to steal it, they were blinded. Those who tried to run away after stealing from the lake were surrounded by the tulip cobras and their venom killed the trespassers within seconds. All these snakes are actually the sons and descendants of a demon,' he concluded.

Shaka interrupted his sermon-like speech, 'Oh! Now here comes another twist. There is a demon, too. Can anybody be more stupid than this?' He chided. But Monty was not in the mood to back down this time. He continued the story that had been narrated to him by the priest of the temple.

'Please listen to what I have to say, and then you all can make a decision. Believe me, I will abide by your decision. I have to die anyway, then why not attempt this? It might be successful. If everything said about the lake and temple is false, then why should there be any hitch to making the biggest haul ever? There indeed was a demon that lived in the weirdest of the weird valley of tulip flowers, aka tulip cobras. It is indeed a strange place with strange things happening all around. Oh, it is so scary that I cannot express my state of mind. I was in the temple when the priest narrated the story of the tulip cobras to me. Had I taken a dip in the holy lake and tried to steal some of the treasure, I would not have been here,' he concluded.

'There is also a room encircled by the seven coloured rocks, which is a part and parcel of the temple. The room has a small ventilator. The demon wakes up at exactly 4 a.m. and, through the rocks, enters the room. At times, even musical instruments can be heard being played, especially during the *amavasya* nights. The demon sleeps in the lake so that no one dares to enter the lake, bathe in it or drink its holy water. All the pilgrims just pray on the shores of the lake, offer some money or something valuable, bow down thrice and leave the sacred place.'

Suleiman laughed at him, 'Monty, you should not get carried away by these superstitious stories. The uneducated villagers often believe anything and everything that is told to them, irrespective of such myths being highly illogical. But tell me, how come no one could steal in such a place? And why do people believe that a demon exists even in these times? They are so dumb and foolish,' he chuckled.

'Boss, I, along with my accomplice, Mehboob, had stolen four paintings from the Roerich Art Gallery situated in a place called Naggar, Raison, near Manali. Later on, we sold all the paintings to a curator for a hefty sum.

'The police got wind of the same and started trailing us. While running from the gallery, one police inspector caught me near the fort of Naggar. There was a scuffle, and the bullet from my revolver pierced his heart. After that incident, both of us ran and took whatever bus was leaving from Raison without realizing that it was going further into the interior, instead of going towards Chandigarh. It went towards this temple and not where we had intended to go. The inspector had instantaneously died, and the entire police force issued a red alert notice for us, but we managed to escape undetected in the local transport bus.

'It dropped us near Chamarel village. In a short while, what we saw was the most breathtaking view of the Himalayan range, the Valley of Flowers, the beautiful lake in the middle of it and a lone temple. The scenic beauty captivated us. The place was uninhabited. Only the temple existed adjacent to the lake. The tulips were strange. All of them, cobra-shaped, were facing the lake, as if ready to strike.

'The villagers, chanting some mantra in their vernacular language, descended towards the temple, while we hid behind the tall *deodar* trees. Later, we saw the villagers offering a gold chain to the demon in the sacred lake. After performing prayers and bowing down before the omnipresent demon, they took the sick child to the priest.

'The priest rubbed some scrub-like thing on the forehead of the child, and in just a few minutes, the sick child got up and seemed to have regained his strength. Even a person like Mehboob got a bit scared on seeing the way the prayers were performed. As if it were some sort of miracle, the sick child managed to somehow get up within minutes and seemed to have recovered from his illness.'

'What about the demon?' questioned Shaka, this time, a little seriously.

'Sir,' Monty continued, 'if you have read the epic Mahabharata, you would know that the five Pandava brothers were sent into exile for twelve long years and one extra year by their cousins, the Kauravas, who had beaten them in a game of dice. The fight between the cousins was for the throne of Hastinapur. The Gita sermon given by Lord Krishna to Arjun and the pitched battle that took place between the Pandavas and Kauravas are all depicted in the epic.'

'I have not read it, but heard these stories from my grandmother umpteen times,' Shaka stated. But Monty, without showing any fear, continued with his story, 'Yes, sir, you may be right, but the epic says that Bhim (the strongest of them) had married Hidamba in Manali. Before that marriage, the five brothers and their single wife, Draupadi, had somehow reached this sacred place. Yudhishthira had ordered the youngest brother to fetch water for them from the lake, the same lake where this demon lived. Sir, it is categorically and vividly mentioned in the epic that one by one, all the brothers were sent to this lake by Yudhishthira to fetch water, but none of them returned. When at last Yudhishthira went to the lake, he found all his brothers lying there in an unconscious state. Before he could understand what had transpired, this demonic crane (a *yaksha*) appeared and asked him to answer one hundred and twenty-five questions correctly if he wanted to live or see his brothers alive again. Yudhishthira, being the wisest of them all, managed to answer all the questions put to him by the demonic crane that claimed to live in the lake and be the guardian of that area. The crane revealed himself to be the god of death, Yama-dharma (yaksha). The crane was satisfied with the answers and allowed them to live and rest there for some time. He allowed them to take the water from the lake. He also forbade his sons, who were masquerading as tulips but in fact were cobras, to harm the Pandavas,' Monty concluded.

Rakesh seemed keenly interested, 'What were the one hundred and twenty-five questions the demon asked King Yudhishthira, and how did he answer those questions put to him by the demonic crane?'

'I do not know how many such children or people will have died in need of proper medical help. What can a bloody priest do or say when a child is sick? He needs medical attention, not musical hymns playing in a temple or the blessings of a so-called demon to get better. You people are nuts!' he stated emphatically. 'If I get my hands on these tantrics, I will kill them all,' he said angrily.

It was Sunder's turn to speak. He was inquisitive, 'One minute, Shaka, let me hear what those one hundred and twenty-five questions and their answers were. That will give us some knowledge too. Let's hear him out. Do you know that there is a place called Nidhivan in the heart of Vrindavan near Mathura? It is said that in Nidhivan, nobody dares to stay during the night. Lord Krishna and his beloved Radha come to life in the said sacred area each night and dance until the wee hours of the morning. Anybody who stays overnight either goes blind or dies, so no one spends even a minute after dusk. When there can be a Nidhivan, that too in the midst of Vrindavan, then why can't there be this temple and lake?' he quipped. Shaka shrugged his shoulders.

He continued, 'Vrindavan, in the literal sense, is a forest full of *tulsi* leaves. At midnight, these tulsi plants turn into *gopis* and dance along with Radha and Lord Krishna throughout the night.' 'Ok, ok, whatever. Now, nobody will further discuss this mythological tale but prepare for the escape,' said Shaka.

Sunder intervened, 'Asking a few questions to Monty is going to be beneficial. I feel that there is no harm in having some knowledge about your destination.'

Monty began explaining, 'You see, all this actually happened in that place now called Maa Kaalimani Temple. The name of the demon was Kaalimani, and that is how the sacred temple got its name. There is no village near that place for the next five kilometres. There are no roads either, just a clay-built pavement which is used by the villagers to reach the temple. Even the villagers travel in a group of at least eight to ten people for the fear of being attacked by wild animals. They, while travelling, play some strange instruments to ward off wild animals such as leopards, wolves, bears, etc.'

'Instead of musical instruments, they should carry a revolver, a .32 calibre, that's what is needed to kill all the animals, the so-called demon and the priest too,' snarled Shaka. Monty retorted, 'Why kill them when they leave by 5 p.m.? There is no one after that till 7 a.m. the next morning.

'No, I want to kill before I steal the treasure, which is purportedly there for the last three thousand years, waiting for Shaka to take it. My fingers are itching too. I have not killed anyone for a long time. I desperately want to smell blood. Let's escape from here and go to that godforsaken place and steal the entire treasure and live like a king thereafter.'

'Let me plan the escape. I am already working on it. Once we are out of this goddamn prison, we will head towards the

Kaalimani Temple, steal the jewellery from the lake and make merry. Do not believe a word Monty has spoken about the people dying there. No one can harm us. We will be carrying enough ammunition,' Shaka stated.

Rakesh agreed wholeheartedly with Shaka and said, 'I can't wait to hold so much jewellery. If the people of that area have false beliefs, what can we do about it? We will spend some time in Manali and then proceed to Kaalimani Temple. After that, I will accompany my leader wherever he intends to go.'

'Manali is also very beautiful,' Monty said, as if in a trance. 'Legend has it that Sage Manu stopped his ark in Manali to create human life after a great deluge had wiped out life in the valley.' Shaka barked back, 'Enough of your mythologies and legends. Let's stick to our guns, Monty.'

But Monty continued as if Shaka were nobody and could not do him the least harm, 'Parikshit, the grandson of Arjun and son of Abhimanyu, had ascended the throne after the Pandavas left. He was killed by Takshak, the serpent king, because Arjun sent an army to burn down this forest infested with snakes.' Shaka gave a push to Monty and said, 'Who were tulips during the day and guarding the treasure at night, right? Oh, stop it, will you?'

Inspite of Shaka's meticulous planning, the escape turned out to be far messier than they had all imagined. It was 31 December 1999, and the tension was palpable with forty-two criminals, some of them hardcore, crammed into the small jail. They avoided looking at each other, staring at the floor, ceiling or anywhere else, but not at each other. They ate bread in silence, as if the imminent doom had cast a dark shadow to chill the air. For the past two months, another inmate and an extortionist, known as Kaku and his gang, had holed up in Jail 16 at the behest of Shaka. They had been digging a tunnel for Shaka and the others to escape. Messages were exchanged surreptitiously with other prisoners who wanted to escape as well.

Kaku, along with Suleiman, led the flock. They stepped down into the tunnel. They would cover the distance of sixty-two feet and open the shaft outside the vast walls of the prison. It would turn out to be the biggest mass escape in the history of Tihar Jail. All of them stepped down one by one. The sudden gust of cold air raised a muffled cheer from the prisoner behind. Kaku and Suleiman stepped out, but they found their excitement a bit premature.

Suleiman, watching the movement of the two sentries in the tower above, clambered out in the open area and tugged a rope, signalling for the exodus to begin. One by one, the escapees silently emerged from the shaft, crawled past the fifty-yard area, and slunk off into the darkness of the jail road and its by-lanes.

Shaka and his companions were out. However, the sentry posted near the shaft noticed some movement and raised an alarm. At least twenty prisoners had already escaped, but another twenty-two were still holed up in the tunnel. They heard the siren and tried to scramble back to the crack, but the tunnel caved in midway. Confusion prevailed in the tunnel. They could neither go back nor go ahead. Panic-stricken, they decided to forge ahead. They came out of the shaft, and the siren started buzzing vociferously. The sentries forged ahead and fired in the darkness, hitting three of the escapees, who fell dead there and then. The others scrambled back to their barracks.

The twelve prisoners who had escaped tried to leave the capital and move in different directions. Five escapees, Suleiman, Shaka, Sunder, Monty, and Rakesh, decided to reach Ambala and split. From Ambala, they travelled by public transport and eventually met at the Hidamba Temple in Manali. Out of forty-two, only eight could finally escape. The other three headed towards Gwalior. They were caught in Agra by an alert sub-inspector, duly informed by the headquarters in Delhi. The massive chase continued; but for Shaka and his gang, all the others were either apprehended or shot dead. Kaku was the last one to face the bullets fired by the Agra police. He was grievously injured and succumbed to his injuries in the Civil Hospital at Agra Cantonment.

Shaka got off the bus at Ropar district (Roopnagar), Punjab, to purchase a revolver and ammunition from an old, country-made pistol manufacturer known to him. All five of them reached Manali and met at the Hidamba Temple on an assigned day, i.e. 4 January 2000. From there, they decided to move further, towards the Kaalimani Temple. It was also the valley where the country's most immense hoard of gold and ornaments was apparently up for grabs. Shaka forbade them from informing anyone of their escape. He trusted no one. They were dressed as mountaineers heading out for a trek, each with a rucksack on their back. They caught the afternoon bus to Raison and got down from the bus after Monty signalled for them to do so. They moved cautiously on the muddy terrain and reached their destination by dusk, unfazed and without encountering any animals or humans on their way. It was very cold, and snow was falling. They found no one travelling through that terrain. Shaka, on reaching the spot, took out his binoculars and looked at the valley. At dusk, the scenery was as pure as it could be. But he was not interested in the scenery. He saw three people. One of them was the head priest, and the other two were helping the priest to close the gates of the Kaalimani Temple. He said to his companions, 'Have they seen us? What is the big hurry? What are they so excited about? Is there something wrong?'

Monty took the binoculars from Shaka and looked at the temple himself. He spoke to himself, 'Where is the fourth one? Last time when I was here, there were four men, who, at sunset, had closed all the doors of the temple before embarking on their daily journey to the nearest village, about five kilometres from here. Boss, how does it matter? Let them run away, and even if they have seen us, how would they know our real purpose? We look like mountaineers.'

Suleiman also retorted, 'Have you seen your face in the mirror? Nobody can tell from a distance that you are anything but a mountaineering enthusiast. Let them go, and then we move in for the kill. Right now, my fingers are itching to shoot these people down. Oh, how much I want to taste blood!' Shaka laughed, 'If we move now, we might have to kill those three coming in this direction. Let them come. Sunder, you tell them that we have lost our way.'

The head priest and the two helpers walked towards them with an expression of men who had seen a ghost. They had no choice but to pass by them because that was the only exit towards their village. Kaalimani Temple and the valley wore a deserted look at that hour. Shaka observed their movement, which was fast-paced. From their nervous expressions, he decided what he should do. While Sunder was asking them about the way to a nearby village, Shaka swiftly took out his dagger and inserted it in the abdomen of the head priest, whose nervousness turned to bewilderment as he fell. The dagger pierced his liver and a part of his stomach. Crimson blood started oozing out from the wound. Shaka struck again, putting an end to the little life that was left in the priest. All were astonished at the ease with which Shaka killed the priest. The two helpers were dumbfounded but gathered enough strength to run for their lives. Sunder threw his knife at one of them. It struck the helper's neck, and blood gushed out of it. He too fell and was lifeless before he touched the ground.

The third person ran for his life, followed by Suleiman. But he stumbled and fell. He gave a last look at his predator before being pounced upon and throttled to death by the burly Suleiman. He used his bare hands to kill the helper within seconds. It was all over within a matter of a few minutes. All three caretakers of the temple were dead. 'The dead do not tell tales,' whispered Shaka. Monty said, 'Was that necessary? We could have easily avoided all that violence. We had come to steal, not to commit murder.'

'Shut up and help us throw these bodies in the river. They knew we had come to commit a heist. It was written large on their faces. Their expressions told me all,' Shaka barked. 'Or was it that you wanted to taste blood and took the decision in haste?' asked Suleiman.

Nobody said anything but helped each other in throwing the three bodies into a deep ravine. After that, they started walking towards the Kaalimani Temple, crossing hundreds of tulip flowers on either side of the path. 'The aura is scary, to say the least,' admitted Suleiman, half-panting. He lifted his rucksack with one hand while holding the blood-soaked knife in the other.

'Let's do our job and leave this place as quickly as we can. This silence is killing me. This place is really weird. Not a soul or even a howl from any animal. Who in their right mind would make a temple here?' muttered Sunder.

Shaka reprimanded him, 'What are you talking about? Are you in your senses? It will take us at least two hours to go down to the bottom of the lake, time and again, to bring up the jewels. The jewels would have scattered and spread all across the bottom of the lake. I do not want to leave even a single item here.'

They crossed over to the temple, which had been closed just a few minutes back by the priest and his assistants, now resting at the bottom of the ravine. The four of them changed into skin-tight costumes that they had arranged through a friend. They wore diving goggles and were carrying torches. One by one, taking a deep breath, they jumped into the lake.

Rakesh kept vigil and had an uncanny feeling that someone, somewhere was observing them. He held the country-made pistol in one hand and a dagger in the other. Two of his accomplices surfaced simultaneously, holding a large number of jewels. They had been down in the lake for only about two minutes. Gold bangles, diamond necklace, bracelets, gold chains and several other ornaments were there for their taking. They placed these valuable items in Suleiman's hand. They had not yet touched the hundred coins lying on the floor of the lake.

Shaka screamed in excitement, 'Man, these superstitious people are crazy! There is a lot more down there than you can imagine. The moment you switch on the torch, they glitter like hell.'

The four people made several trips down the lake, and each trip was worth a haul. Rakesh kept accumulating the ornaments with a grin. He was so much engrossed in counting the numerous jewels that it was too late when he heard the sound of hissing and came face to face with imminent death. Two snakes bit him, one on his neck and one on his left calf, and he died within seconds, holding the jewels in his hand and with a horrified expression on his face. It was growing dark, and as if pre-planned, the snakes moved back towards the seven coloured rocks and swiftly went inside a pit, leaving the dead body just on the bank of the lake.

Sunder looked alarmed when he came out of the lake and saw Rakesh lying dead on the bank. Shaka inspected the two bites, one on the neck, the other on the left calf, and realized they were indeed snakebites. It was yet another moonless night and it was pitch dark by then. The torches that they held in their hands were the only source of light. By now, several ornaments worth a fortune were packed up in their rucksacks.

Shaka stated matter-of-factly, 'We cannot do anything about Rakesh. Let us find some wood and light a fire to ward off any animals or snakes, for that matter.' Sunder said sarcastically, 'Well, Rakesh died because he wanted us to split the jewels into four parts.'

Shaka and Sunder got hold of a few tree branches and built a fire. They were all shocked to see more than a hundred snakes slithering towards them from the side of the lake, where the tulip flowers were planted. 'Have those goddamn tulips actually transformed into cobras?' yelled Shaka.

The four of them indulged in indiscriminate firing and shot dead nearly thirty snakes moving towards them. Some snakes backed off and crawled towards the bushes, while some kept attacking. Suleiman lost his balance and fell. Before he could refill the cartridges in his revolver, several snakes bit him, and life drained out of him. Sunder, Shaka and Monty ran towards the road, leaving the rucksacks on the pavement. They were scared to death. Killing innocent unarmed people was one thing, but facing hundreds of cobras was another.

Sunder stumbled and fell. His pistol and torch fell with him. Within seconds, a horde of cobras was on him, sinking their fangs into him. Monty and Shaka, the only two left, ran towards the small room they had seen on their way to the lake. They desperately wanted to save themselves from an unimaginably horrible assault by the cobras. Monty gave Shaka an 'I told you so!' look.

Before they could reach the room, they noticed some movement behind the trees. Shaka fired at the lock and pushed the door open. It was pitch dark inside the room. Both of them hurriedly entered the dark room and shut the door before hundreds of snakes could kill them. It was an empty room, not even a shred of cloth, wood or, for that matter, anything at all was present.

The sound of hissing reminded them that the snakes were gathering outside the room. Then suddenly, the hissing stopped. Shaka and Monty waited with bated breath. They wondered what was happening outside. Were they turning back into tulip flowers? Was their assault over? Would they be able to survive this ordeal?

Suddenly, in that eerie silence, there was a knock on the door—a gentle knock. Monty was about to open the bolt when Shaka asked him to hold on for a minute. He wanted to check first. A hardened criminal was always cautious. 'Who is it?' he yelled. No reply came from outside, and again an eerie silence enveloped them. There was another knock on the door. Shaka signalled his accomplice not to open the door. He wanted to double-check. He opened the ventilator and saw a boy in his teens, knocking at the door.

He was a good-looking, slim boy, wearing leopard skin on his torso. It looked strange, but the boy seemed innocent enough and was staring at Shaka. The teenager who was just staring at them was probably just a boy who had lost his way and was looking for shelter, Shaka thought. But then, where the hell did the cobras vanish? Was he some God in a teenage avatar come to help them out? Monty also peeped out and saw the boy. He whispered to Shaka, 'He is the demon. Don't go by his innocent face. The snakes have disappeared because of the arrival of the demon. He will kill us for sure.'

Shaka looked at him in dismay, 'You silly bugger. If he were a demon, why would he knock at the door? He is only a child and has either come to help us out of this situation or to seek shelter like us.'

'Open up. I will aim this revolver at him. One wrong move and I will riddle him with bullets,' he snarled. Monty went ahead and opened the door. The innocent boy stared at the two killers and slowly walked inside the room.

Shaka spoke, pointing the gun at him, 'Who are you and what do you want?' The boy suddenly bent down and gave a scary howl—the howl of a wolf. He was a wolf in sheep's skin. From nowhere, a pack of wolves—some twelve of them—emerged from behind the nearby bushes and leapt inside, red eyes and saliva dripping from their mouths filled with sharp teeth.

The torch from Shaka's hand fell as he saw the ferocious wolves entering the room at the behest of the innocent-looking boy. The wolves charged at them. Shaka fired, but it was too late. Four of them attacked and pinned both the criminals to the floor. The boy raised his hands, the fingers showing curled up nails as if they had not been cut for a long time. His nails looked more like claws. This time Shaka could sense a different kind of howl.

He howled once again. It was almost a shriek. Instantaneously, the wolves, using their sharp teeth, inflicted fatal wounds on the bodies of Shaka and Monty, who, as it is, had surrendered to their fate. Within seconds, all the other wolves came in and devoured the lifeless bodies of the two intruders who had dared to steal the treasures.

At 7 a.m., some villagers and pilgrims came down towards the valley. There was no trace of the five bodies, not even a bone or a mark of blood was visible. It was as if the five criminals who had dared to steal the forbidden treasure had been rendered extinct.

The boy had quietly thrown the jewellery, along with their rucksack and belongings and their guns and revolvers into the deepest part of the lake. The pack of wolves had left after a hearty meal. The tulip flowers were in their complete splendour; unfurling their petals, they were guarding the lake and the treasures therein.

Police found the bodies of the priest and his two aides floating in Beas River. After an investigation was conducted, the police closed the case file after filing murder charges against unknown persons. The police also found a large pit near the seven coloured rocks and a clump of tulips near which they found several murdered cobras. Another priest was appointed and the temple was again filled with music. That night, the innocent boy had saved the temple and its treasure.

REVOLUTIONARY GURU

It was a bright afternoon on 13 April 1919. Master Tara Singh, a tall, bearded, turban-clad Sikh, was delivering his patriotic speech at Jallianwala Bagh in Amritsar, Punjab. He was in his true element. His words were persuasive, exhorting the audience to make a final call for the attainment of freedom from British rule, which Indians had endured for over a century and a half. The British rulers were not only uncouth but had also been unscrupulous enough to pillage and plunder India's wealth. Over the past one and a half centuries, they had wreaked havoc on the people and stripped the country of its vast resources.

A large, peaceful crowd had gathered on the day of Baisakhi to protest the Rowlatt Act. Master Tara Singh spoke in a mixture of Punjabi and Hindi, with a tone full of hatred and disdain for the cruel British rulers of India. Without any fear of the mighty British Empire, he asserted, 'Dear brothers and sisters of our motherland, we firmly believe that mass cruelties like passing the Rowlatt Act are designed to switch off the intellectual capacities of Indians and make us live like rotten mangoes. The people of our country will not be willing to accept the magical simplifications and let the British ravage India. The days of slavery at the hands of the wicked Britishers are now numbered. We shall rise against the British by uniting to fight for our freedom. It will require hard work, determination, defiance and tenacity. A nation as diverse as ours and having a population of around thirty crores cannot be subject to the brutalities of these seventy thousand Britishers.'

People started clapping frantically, and there were loud shouts of '*Bharat mata ki jai*', and 'Down with imperialism'. Amongst the gathering was a seven-year-old, Ram Kumar, holding his father Dev Dutt's hand with his tiny fingers; he had come to participate in the congregation. With him was also his nine-year-old elder brother, Sukhdev. He could hardly understand the meaning of the strong speech. The sun was about half an hour away from setting. It was around 5 p.m., Master Tara Singh was speaking to the now emotionally-charged people of Amritsar, who wanted to achieve freedom at any cost. The leader continued to talk, 'The war ended last year; however, the price of the protracted war in money and workforce has been enormous. High causality rates, inflation, compounded by heavy taxation, and the deadly 1918 pandemic have all escalated our sufferings at the hands of the British. After that, Sidney Rowlatt has been instrumental in passing the Rowlatt Act, which we vehemently oppose. It restricts our civil liberties. A few days ago, twenty thousand people gathered for a protest march in Anarkali Bazar, Lahore. Dear countrymen and fellow citizens, on 10 April 1919, we had protested at the residence of Miles Irving, the Deputy Commissioner of Amritsar, for the release our leaders, Satya

Pal and Saifuddin Kitchlew. Two days back, on 11 April, English missionary Marcella Sherwood was assaulted in Kucha Kurrichhan Street. We condemn such violence. Our leaders present here, such as Hans Raj, Lal Kanhyalal Bhatia, held a meeting yesterday at Hindu College, Dhabi Khatikan. There, it was decided that a peaceful protest meeting would be held here at Jallianwala Bagh.'

People were keenly listening to the speech at the Jallianwala Bagh, a garden complex which was adjacent to the Golden Temple and Harminder Sahib. The Jallianwala Bagh had only one narrow entrance and a well right in the centre of the park. The entry as well as the exit was through one narrow gate only.

Dev Dutt was listening to the speech intently. Dev Dutt's family comprised his wife, Damyanti, and three sons: Sukhdev, Ram and Shiv. They had never been a part of the freedom movement. On the contrary, Dev Dutt was a constable in the British police, posted at the Sardar Thana police station. While Damyanti and Shiv had stayed at home, Dev Dutt had taken his two sons, Sukhdev and Ram, to the Golden Temple to celebrate Baisakhi. While merely passing through Jallianwala Bagh, he had decided to join the audience who were listening to the vociferous patriotic speeches being delivered by the leaders of the Congress Party. Though a constable in the British police, he held a burning desire to attain freedom.

Master Tara Singh continued to speak to the cheering crowd about freedom, which had to be snatched from the cruel British rulers' claws. He continued, 'My dear brothers and sisters, these are not ordinary times. Ordinary people cannot understand extraordinary circumstance prevailing in the country. We must make extraordinary efforts to throw these wretched rulers out of our country. Unknown to Master Tara Singh, and the Congress leaders and the family of Dev Dutt who were in true Baisakhi Festival mood, Col. Reginald Dyer, the acting military commander of Amritsar, had arranged for an airplane to fly over Jallianwala Bagh to estimate the size of the crowd which had gathered. He had received a report from the Commissioner that the crowd had swelled up to around fifteen thousand. Col. Dyer was unhappy at the ever-increasing number of people listening to the anti-British speeches that were being delivered that day at Jallianwala Bagh.

Dev Dutt stood with his two sons in the central part of the park, near the large well partly filled with water. Suddenly, at around 5:30 p.m., Dev Dutt turned his head and noticed Col. Dyer and a group of fifty troops armed with .303 Lee–Enfiled bolt action rifles taking position. He was a trained police man. He immediately understood the next intended course of action. He hurriedly gathered his two sons and started to run towards the sole exit, when suddenly a hail of bullets struck the wall next to him. Without warning the crowd to disperse, Col. Dyer had ordered his troops to open fire. A bullet grazed his right arm, resulting in Ram Kumar and him falling. Sukhdev continued to run towards the exit. The troops continued to fire at the innocent people for ten minutes, using around two thousand cartridges. Around fifteen hundred people were injured, and around a thousand people were killed, which included forty-two boys, of whom the youngest was seven months old. While the nine-year-old Sukhdev was trying to run towards the exit, several bullets had hit him.

He had died instantaneously. The nine-year-old lay dead amongst the heap of bodies strewn all over Jallianwala Bagh. Dev Dutt had been injured; he and his younger son had fallen down, which had kept them out of the way of the bullets unleashed by Col. Dyer.

Another few yards, and Sukhdev would have exited the park, but God had decided to snatch him away on that fateful day. God had not been kind to the thousands of innocent people who had gathered in the park that day.

Dev Dutt searched for his younger son, who was hiding behind the well's wall. He lifted the dead body of Sukhdev, and while tears were rolling down his cheeks, he took him to the nearby hospital, where he was declared dead. Ram Kumar was in a state of shock and he had lost his voice. The sound of the firing of bullets had echoed so much so that he had also temporarily lost his sense of hearing. His vocal cords refused to respond. He had witnessed many women with children of tender age jumping into the well and drowning.

The seven-year-old Ram Kumar too was feeling intense grief. The sight of his father carrying his elder brother's body was going to be embedded in his mind for all time to come.

Dev Dutt realized that life would never be the same for his younger son after that traumatic experience. One moment his elder brother was alive, and the next, he was gone forever. Ram had always looked up to his elder brother for help, support and guidance. The brutal death of his elder brother shook his foundations and left a huge, frightening void in his life.

The massacre at Jallianwala Bagh led to widespread rage. Dev Dutt cursed Col. Dyer and the British for unleashing terror on the innocent natives for no fault of theirs. It took a while for his son to recover and regain his hearing and speech. However, whenever he spoke, a stutter persisted. Dev Dutt resigned from the service of the British. He took up a minor job as a security guard at a bank located on Mall Road, Amritsar. He, too, opposed Col. Dyer for his ruthless, unethical and shameless behaviour.

Ram grew up to be a recluse, an introvert who isolated himself from society. He had been a good student at the government school in Amritsar but always preferred to be a loner. He read articles about Bhagat Singh, Udham Singh and Chandrashekhar Azad, but seldom discussed their sacrifices with his father, Dev Dutt, and younger brother, Shiv Kumar.

Time passed, and the freedom struggle had settled down in Punjab by the 1930s. Ram had become a graduate and was preparing to take the civil services exams. His parents wanted him to lead a normal, everyday life, but Ram remained shut up in his room—far away from the everyday life they wanted for him. His father would often ask him not to take the civil services exam, as that would require him to serve the British rulers.

On the recommendation of the Superintendent of Police Thomas Rose, Ram Kumar got a job as a junior division clerk in the Public Works Department. He continued his studies to clear the civil services exam.

By 1933, Ram was twenty years old and had developed a good height and a muscular body. His bodybuilding exercise had borne good results. He was a typical Punjabi youngster.

Ram, being an introvert, was attracted to Madhumati, a neighbour, who had grown up to be a lovely girl. She had a fair complexion, big eyes, and long, black hair. She wasn't tall, but she held herself in style, with her hair parted in the centre and kohl in her eyes. She could not afford gold earrings, but, as Ram saw, she always wore artificial earrings.

Ram had completed his graduation and had bought a bicycle for himself. On one pretext or the other, he would follow Madhumati from her college to her house and then resume his duties at the government department. Everyone affectionately called Madhumati 'Madhu'. She was well-aware of his intentions but had preferred to ignore him. She considered him a weakling, despite his strong body and personality—someone who was too shy and would never muster the courage to speak to her.

In her heart of hearts, she did not appreciate his government job. On the contrary, she was enamoured by freedom fighters such as Bhagat Singh and Chandra Shekhar Azad, who had the courage to face the torture of the Britishers. One person that she truly admired was the unknown crusader of Amritsar, who, of late, had been held responsible for the killings of several British soldiers. The British had even announced a prize of ten thousand rupees for any information about this lone crusader, who they were calling Black Panther. It was rumoured that the Black Panther had killed the Superintendent of Police Thomas Rose, while he was on his way to the police station.

Dev Dutt learned from a neighbour that Ram was interested in Madhu, as her beauty had smitten him. He was also aware that it was a one-sided romance. What he was not aware of was the fact that Madhu too had started looking forward to Ram's visits to her college with pleasurable anticipation.

In the meantime, Germany's soldiers had marched into Poland and Czechoslovakia and captured the province in northern Czechoslovakia without bloodshed, causing immense shame, discomfort and embarrassment to the other European countries. While Europe was reeling under the threat of a world war, orchestrated by Adolf Hitler, British India was facing a massive upsurge led by Subhash Chandra Bose and Gandhi ji to gain freedom.

The killings in Punjab continued unabated. In the next three months, several British officers were killed by unknown gunmen. The modus operandi was somewhat the same. Someone with his face covered in a monkey cap would emerge on a motorcycle, shoot the British victims and leave the crime scene before anyone could apprehend him. He at times wore a mask with a design resembling a panther's face. The killer became famous as Black Panther and the natives, including Madhu, started eulogizing him. Though Gandhi ji and Nehru condemned such killings, Subhash Chandra Bose showered praises on the lone crusader. The British commanding officer was furious. He ordered the arrest and death of the perpetrator of these killings. He gave shoot-at-sight orders even if the evidence was not fully against any culprit. Just a hint of coming to know that a rebel had, or might have, some hand in these killings would be sufficient for them to be shot at sight. The law suddenly changed its colour, and no questions could be asked if a trigger-happy Major Smith killed some natives on mere conjecture.

Whilst Britishers were being killed one by one and the frequency of the same was increasing by the day, Ram Kumar was getting more and more involved with Madhu. His advances were being responded to positively by his beloved, who had started meeting him. They began meeting at various secluded parks and places. But once when she asked him to meet her at Jallianwala Bagh, he refused point-blank. He would never enter that Bagh ever. He still had hallucinations of the massacre. Madhu considered him a coward and too weak-minded for refusing to enter Jallianwala Bagh. She did not appreciate Ram Kumar's timid behaviour and his being oblivious to the ongoing freedom struggle.

However, with the passage of time, his patience and persistence resulted in her agreeing to marry him. Dev Dutt and Damyanti were informed about the alliance, and they gladly accepted the proposal forwarded by Madhu's Parents, who had visited their house with one kilo of jaggery and a one-rupee note.

Suddenly, the two households had positive vibrations, laughter, and numerous relatives and friends visiting the two families on and off. The environment had changed for the better, and there was merriment in Dev Dutt's house after a long interval. The incident that happened on 13 April 1919 was forgotten. Arrangements were now being made for the arrival of a new family member. Lengthy streamers of flowers were put up and the house of Dev Dutt in Sandhu Colony was lit up with bulbs and decorative items.

Damyanti was excited to have a good-looking daughter-in-law in her house. She was eager for her to come to her home since she only had sons. She was looking forward and was happy because she had massive apprehensions about Ram Kumar's capabilities. He was not only a weakling, but was as timid as one could be. He would not harm even a fly, and girls in Amritsar did not favour having such simpletons and weaklings as their husbands. There was no machismo in her son and she had doubts about his masculinity. It was enough for her that Ram Kumar was finally getting married and would settle down in life.

The priest was called from the nearby Laxmi Narayan Temple. Since the stars were not favourable after 30 September 1939, the marriage had to be solemnised on that very date, which fell only a fortnight later.

Ram sent a message through his younger brother, Shiv, to Madhu, asking her to meet him at the terrace of her house. He could easily jump from one terrace to another to reach her terrace. During the summer, however, such shenanigans were not possible as almost every resident slept on their respective terraces.

But winter had almost arrived and people had started sleeping indoors. At the assigned time, he reached the rendezvous point to find Madhu already awaiting his arrival. He caressed her for the first time to which she did not object. 'Madhu,' he whispered, 'now nobody in this world can create any hurdle in our union. You were mine and shall be mine forever. I have always dreamt of you as being my bride. Tomorrow we shall tie the nuptial knot and be together forever.'

Madhu stated, 'I know, but Jai Chand is quite unhappy with our alliance.' He replied, 'Oh, that general merchant's son, he can do nothing. He may be a rich man's son and his father may be a loyal servant of the British, but I swear I will not let anyone come between you and me. If anyone even so much as tries, I will kill him with my bare hands.' He emphasized the word kill and was quite stern in his approach towards Jai Chand.

She came closer to him and said, 'Oh! I am seeing another side of your personality. I thought I was marrying a person who can never be assertive. But I love you and am willing to do anything for you.' Ram gently kissed her, and his response was far greater than she had expected. 'Madhu, remember, when people believe in you, it gives you motivation, but when you believe in yourself, it gives determination and infinite energy.' Madhu raised her eyebrows and said, 'Oh my God! Who are you? I am beginning to have doubts about you. I thought I was marrying a clerk in the government who was living a solitary life without any motivation. I am pleasantly surprised at the change in your demeanour. You have always been a mute, silent person.' With a beam, Ram stated, 'No sound in the world can be louder than your silence. If you will not understand my silence, you will never be able to understand my words. Every changing colour of a leaf is beautiful. Changing situations of life are meaningful. One needs a clear vision. If you are marrying me, you must know that I do intend to do something extraordinary as was done by Sardar Udham Singh, or as was said by Master Tara Singh way back in 1919.'

He paused and then said, 'I intend to reveal something tomorrow on our wedding night. It is always better to reveal secrets at an opportune time.' She giggled, 'Oh, I love secrets, but I will not be able to sleep tonight. You must reveal that secret now; you know women are always inquisitive by nature.'

There was a long pause and then he said, 'I am the Black Panther, the lone crusader.' Both of them caressed each other.

He realized that this time the desire to hold him was greater in Madhu. She grimaced, 'Waheguru, I should have guessed that behind that timid Ram was the man of my dreams.' Ram replied, 'Sometimes the weight we need to lose isn't on our body.' Madhu kept her palm on his lips, 'Say nothing, my love! I am eager to be with you forever. You know that I used to keep a fast on each Monday and wish that my husband would be somewhat like the Black Panther, but I could never have thought that my husband would turn out to be the Black Panther.' They then kissed each other goodbye.

The next day, Ram and Madhumati were supposed to tie the knot. It was the wedding day, and the Punjabis were eager to utilize the opportunity to sing songs and make merry.

Dev Dutt had ensured that eatables and local beverages were in free flow. After all, it was his son's wedding and an occasion to be celebrated with aplomb albeit within his means. It had taken a week or so to paint and whitewash the house and polish the furniture. He had taken a loan from the bank, courtesy of his manager, and the old, beleaguered security guard, who was about to retire, was looking forward to the marriage of his reclusive son.

Ram Kumar was on cloud nine, totally oblivious to the approaching events. It was a bit chilly on 30 September morning, but later in the day, bright sunshine cleared the fog which had engulfed the sky for a short while. There were at least two dozen relatives in Ram Kumar's small house in Sandhu Colony. Ram was engrossed in his thoughts about Madhu—his Madhu.

His cousin Sushmita tapped his shoulder and remarked a bit teasingly, 'Brother, are you still dreaming about Madhumati?

Wake up and get ready for the turmeric ceremony. I will cover your face and arms with so much turmeric that you will not be able to recognize yourself.' With a tinge of embarrassment, he replied, 'Dear sister, is it my day or yours? I am getting married, and I will lay down the rules.'

A sumptuous breakfast, with typical Punjabi cuisine, was laid out on the tables—lots of sweets made in pure ghee and several other dishes. A number of ceremonies were performed, and more and more relatives and friends kept on being ushered into the house to celebrate the occasion.

At around 4 p.m., the priest performed the ceremony and prayed to God while adorning the *sehra* on him. Ram Kumar was beaming with happiness and looking handsome in the bridegroom's attire. His beloved Madhu would be betrothed to him.

Suddenly, two police jeeps and one police van, each carrying around ten police officers, entered the lane of Sandhu Colony. It was a scary sight. The band stopped abruptly. Neighbours came out of their houses to witness the large contingent of police led by Major Smith. Covering the house of Dev Dutt, Smith entered the house with a revolver in his hand and shouted, 'Stop the ceremonies. Right now!'

Dev Dutt came forward and asked, 'Sir, what's wrong. I do not understand at all. We have done nothing wrong, sir. We are in the midst of a wedding ceremony. The *baraat* has to leave for the bride's house in half an hour.'

Smith looked up at Ram Kumar and said, 'Ram Kumar, your game is up. We have received information from Jai Chand and confiscated the motorcycle used by you to commit all those killings of the police officers in Amritsar, Jalandhar,

Ludhiana, Moga, etc.' He turned to Ram Kumar's father and said triumphantly, 'Mr Dutt, he has been masquerading as the Black Panther, and there is prize money of ten thousand rupees on his head. He will come with me to the police station. Jai Chand had been following him, and the other night, when Ram Kumar took out a motorcycle from an old, vacant haunted house, Jai Chand had followed him. He had killed Sir Thomas and returned to the same dilapidated old house and parked his motorcycle.'

Ram Kumar's father exclaimed, 'Sir, you are absolutely incorrect in your insinuations. My son has never gone outside Amritsar, leave aside other places. He doesn't even go to Jallianwala Bagh.' Dev Dutt and Damyanti too intervened and pleaded with folded hands, 'Sir, I request you to please reconsider your decision. I have always detested his going to the company garden to try and catch butterflies. But, anybody in their right mind would have to be out of their mind to level such serious charges against my son.'

Smith had his revolver aimed at Ram Kumar. He shifted his stance and spoke aloud, 'You old foolish woman, you do not know your son well enough. He has created this image. All over the colony people think that he is a coward, timid boy who lacks courage, gets easily frightened. No, you imbecile brainless morons, you bloody browns are all mistaken! All of you present here are stupid, half-witted, dunces and doltish in the truest sense. Do not try to stop me from performing my duties, or else I will be compelled to shoot you down too. Even people in Lahore and Rawalpindi have started to ape him. He is the most dangerous man and the most wanted terrorist in Punjab Suba. Though he was a lone crusader, Jai Chand has got the better of him, and Ram Kumar will be tried in court and hanged to death.'

Whilst Ram remained quiet and still, Shiv came forward and said politely, 'Sir, my brother cannot be a killer by any stretch of imagination. For more than fifteen years, we have been sleeping, studying and playing in the same room. There is not even an iota of evidence that he is the Black Panther. There is no possibility of him being the person who has taken to violence and dispensed with Gandhi ji's philosophy of non-violence and civil disobedience.'

'You naïve boy, do not interfere. While he claims to be a follower of Gandhi, he actually follows the path laid down by that Bengali, Subhash Chandra Bose. It was none other than your brother who shot Sir Thomas Rose dead, steered the van robbery, and killed Johnston and his wife Maria outside the Gymkhana club. Till now, this "innocent" man has killed seventeen British officers and conducted several robberies. He is the most wanted terrorist in North India. People eulogize Black Panther and await news of his exploits in Amritsar. We know how you bloody Indians smile when another British officer is killed by this scoundrel of a man. Ram! Hands up! Surrender, otherwise I have orders to shoot you.'

Sushmita gathered courage and said, 'If my brother is the Black Panther, then hats off to him, and we salute him. You can do whatever you want, but from this day on, we will all admire him. He is our Bhagat Singh and a true patriot. Many in this country are "*todhi bachaas*", cowards who lick the shoes of the British. My brother, I bow before you for your courage, bravery and patriotism. If you are the Black Panther, then we are all proud of you.'

Suddenly, Shiv moved and held Smith from behind using his strong arm. Smith fired, and the bullet hit Dev Dutt in his chest. Ram Kumar threw his sehra and ran towards his room. The other policeman, realizing the precarious situation, started firing, indiscriminately injuring Damyanti and Sushmita grievously.

Ram Kumar came out of his room, brandishing a country-made revolver. He fired at Smith, and the bullet pierced his right eye and hit the wall behind him. Shiv remained unscathed but in immense shock as the body of Smith slumped down lifelessly. Ram yelled, 'This is the eighteenth one, and if I have to kill all seventy thousand of them, I will do so.'

There was mayhem in the courtyard as bullets were fired from both sides. Ram was not one to bow down before the police force. He went all guns blazing and killed four constables besides Smith. The indiscriminate firing by then had taken the lives of two more members of the family, Shiv and Sushmita. Both had taken a hail of bullets and were dead before they even hit the ground. Dev Dutt had lost too much blood. Life drained out of his body, and his pupils became still. Five from the British force and seven other people, including three neighbours, also died in the melee.

In the span of a few minutes, Ram had lost his father, brother and cousin sister. While continuing to fire at the police contingent, he jumped out from the side window and ran towards Jallianwala Bagh. Over there, he once again hid behind the well, which was located in the central part of the park. He had done the same thing on 13 April 1999 when his elder brother had collapsed and died.

He checked his revolver and the belt that he carried with him. There were only two bullets left in the revolver, which he had reloaded, and around seven cartridges in the belt. He quickly reloaded the country-made revolver and waited for the police officers.

The British Resident Commissioner sent another force of fifty paramilitary men to arrest the Panther alive. He was too important to kill without knowing about his support and the people behind his concerted assault against the British. Or did he really work alone?

Once again, forces armed to the teeth with rifles and machine guns entered from the small alley of the infamous Jallianwala Bagh. They encircled him from all corners, and he was instructed to surrender. Finding himself in a dire and hopeless situation, he threw away the revolver and surrendered before the paramilitary force.

A huge crowd had gathered outside the Jallianwala Bagh. As he was handcuffed and taken to the Amritsar Central Prison in an open jeep, the people of Amritsar showered petals upon him and raised the slogan of 'Long live, Panther; long live, Panther'. Madhumati with tears of joy in her eyes was one of those who showered petals upon him.

Black Panther, on the last count, had been responsible for killing at least twenty-one government traitors. He had to wait for the inevitable verdict by the British Judge who would certainly sentence him to death.

However, the crowd, which swelled from nearby villages to have a glimpse of the anonymous Panther's face, turned into a law-and-order situation. Thousands of people took out a protest march and chanted his pseudonym. Posters with his face and a panther's face printed on the background were put up everywhere. This poster was pasted on many government and private buildings and on the walls of Amritsar.

The government, finding it extremely difficult to control the situation created by this revaluation, shifted him to the Andaman and Nicobar Islands prison. While his case was to be heard by a judge in court he would remain incarcerated there. Gandhi and Nehru condemned his tactics, but Subhash Chandra Bose praised him. Subhash Chandra Bose, in one of his speeches, had said, 'Rise, fellow Indian, rise as the Black Panther has risen. Do not fear facing failure in your attempts. Even successful mathematicians start with a zero. Our Panther scored twenty-one. I salute him. My fellow citizen, you can never evaluate your potential unless you join the race for freedom like the Panther.'

A patriotic group called Azadi Sangh had printed posters of the Panther, Dev Dutt and Shiv and put them up on the walls in Calcutta, Patna, Bhubaneshwar and Amritsar. Black Panther had become a rage and an ideal.

Overnight, Ram Kumar had become a hero who had very ardently followed in the footsteps of Shahid Bhagat Singh and Netaji Subhash Chandra Bose. He had taken to violence and killed the cruel Britishers all by himself. His quote, as stated by the court, became famous. He had replied to the Judge by saying that, 'Tough times are like physical exercises. You may find it tough when you are doing them, but you emerge stronger because of them. Jai Hind.'

The Council of Britain wanted to hang him or kill him in an encounter, but to make him a martyr would have created another law-and-order situation. But, as the days passed, the protesters were reduced to a handful of men, and on Subhash Chandra Bose leaving for Germany, the unflinching support of the Panthers frittered down to nought. The British had turned out to be successful once again.

Torture and death by starvation were a common feature of the Cellular Jail on Andaman Island. It was rumoured that Chattar Singh was tortured for three years by being suspended in an iron suit. Mahavir Singh and many other prisoners had died due to being force-fed.

Some time back, 238 prisoners at the Cellular Jail had attempted to escape. All of them were caught in one go, and eighty-seven of them were hanged and executed. The British officers were brutal and did not bat an eyelid before hanging a freedom fighter.

The Cellular Jail was located at Port Blair in the Southern Andaman Islands of the Bay of Bengal and was also known as Kala Pani. The prison was built in such a way that the sea surrounded the prison complex. It was impossible to escape from the newly constructed and renovated prison.

When Ram Kumar was brought to the prison, there was a lot of excitement. The inmates shouted his name as he walked, duly chained, towards his cell. 'Long live the Panther,' shouted the inmates. His popularity had spread to most parts of India.

Most of the prisoners were tortured for information by the jail superintendent, Barry. While in prison, Ram met famous patriots during the half-hour breaks, such as Veer Savarkar, Batukeshwar Dutt, Sudhanshu Das Gupta, and others. He was impressed by the views expressed by Sushil Das Gupta, the president of the Jugantar Party. He was a freedom fighter from the Wahabi movement. The Manipur Revolutionaries were also imprisoned in the Cellular Jail at the Andaman and Nicobar Islands.

Savarkar, in one of his interactions with Ram Kumar, while both were working to make coconut oil for the authorities, had told him that the design of the Cellular Jail was heavily influenced by the model of the panopticon: a circular structure, with a revolving centre, where the guard would be housed. It would allow a single person to keep watch on all the prisoners from the central tower because prisoners would regulate their own behaviour, believing themselves to be constantly observed, even when they are not.

Once, on being tortured, Ram Kumar lost a lot of blood and fainted. The doctors informed Jailer Barry that he needed medical attention and would have to be taken to a hospital situated at Port Blair. The senior had given instructions to not to make a martyr of him.

Jailor Barry had given Ram the task of pounding coconuts to produce a back-breaking quota of fibres. When Ram could not meet the desired quota, Barry raised his whip and started beating him along, while letting loose a torrent of abuse. Barry saw to it that prison would be a living hell for the prisoners, even while he and other British officers lived in style at Ross Island. Ram Kumar had fainted and had to be hospitalized due to excessive injuries.

While he was being taken on a boat to Port Blair, he feigned unconsciousness and, seizing an opportunity, jumped into the Bay of Bengal. By the time it was noticed that he was not on the deck, he had swum afar, across to a nearby isolated island.

Ram knew that the jailer would come looking for him,

and the punishment would be a bullet between his eyes. He rested for half an hour and again swam to yet another nearby Island. He had no idea about the demography of the area but had gathered information that there were, in all, 572 islands, and most of them were uninhabited. The Bay of Bengal was the world's largest bay, geographically.

Ram would rest for a couple of hours and then again venture to yet another island. He was least bothered about the sharks or the unbearable waves of the Bay of Bengal. They were nothing compared to the unscrupulous David Barry.

Ram Kumar could survive the torture unleashed by Barry and the ordeal of swimming in the ocean all by himself simply because he wanted to live to fight against the Britishers. There was also another reason for his will to survive—Madhu's face came before his eyes every time he lost the will to survive.

He finally decided to settle on a deserted island far away from the Cellular Jail. There was no one on that small island. Only some birds and vegetation were his company. He drank coconut water and ate fruits to quench his thirst and assuage his appetite.

Once, while he was still alone in the godforsaken island and was living on coconuts for survival, he saw two British motorboats on the shore. He rushed to the other side of the island which had a dense forest. He kept on hiding till sunset dawned upon the island. When he came out, the two ships had left, and there was no sign of Barry or his henchmen, who, in fact, had been frantically looking for him.

Ram found a cave deep inside the island that protected him from the wild animals. Gradually, he improvised and made a bow and an arrow for himself. Using a net made of plants, he could catch some fish in the bay and satisfy his hunger better. Unknown to him, the British, at home, had been facing massive attacks and bombardments from Adolf Hitler's Luftwaffe.

Ram Kumar lived on that island for the next couple of weeks, when he again noticed three boats with Japanese markings harbouring on its shores. He knew that he could rely upon any other community but the British. He had recognized the Nippon flag from afar.

He ran towards them, waving a white flag, kept for precisely this purpose. The captain of this ship was a Japanese man named Yokumata. He had been assigned the task of establishing a base in an island near Port Blair and use the same later on to launch attacks on the British. On realizing that the man waving the white flag was a freedom fighter who had remained a prisoner at the infamous Cellular Jail, Yokumata took him aboard.

Ram Kumar gave him a lot of information about the British torturing the freedom fighters at the Cellular Jail and the army and forces stationed there. That information was helpful for the Japanese captain Yokumata.

The captain of the Japanese ship was courteous enough to drop Ram Kumar at the seaport of Thislawa Harbour in Burma. Ram Kumar thanked him profusely and walked towards Yangon. Amritsar was around 2000 miles from Yangon. He had to find a way to reach his hometown. His bearded look made him unrecognizable. He had also developed a white streak in his hair and looked older than his age.

He had not realized that he had spent a long period in prison and on the islands, and the years had passed; he came to know about the world and the adverse events that had taken place in the meantime. He came to know of Rabindranath Tagore and Gandhi ji, of the fact that independence was just a few months away, since World War II, which was on, had weakened the British Empire and hurt it where it hurt them most. He made enquiries in Yangon and found, to his utter surprise, that there was a Gurudwara at Insein Phyu Road, Yangon. It was known as Insein Sikh Temple. He was in a bad state but knew that the Gurudwara not only offered shelter but a free langar open to all sects of society.

He entered the Gurudwara and informed the *granthi*s that he was from Amritsar, the holy land of the Golden Temple. Sardar Santokh Singh, the head granthi, was overwhelmed on meeting someone from his hometown. Ram wore a turban and requested Sardar Santokh Singh to record his name in the register maintained at the Gurudwara as Ram Singh. Jathendar acceded to his request, and Ram Kumar became Ram Singh, an identity he needed to reach Amritsar. He was desperate to reach Amritsar and meet his mother, Madhu and other relatives. He was desperate to tell them that he was very much alive.

He worked relentlessly at the Gurudwara, saved some money from the salary which he earned, and after spending a couple of weeks over there, he left for Amritsar. It took him several days to reach the railway junction at Amritsar. The moment he got down at the Amritsar railway station, he bent down and touched the mother earth of his hometown. A lot had changed. His mother had passed away and so had Madhu's parents. His house had been sealed by the British. The enquiries revealed that Madhu had been married off to someone far away. He was devastated. His journey to Amritsar had been full of excitement and anxiety, but the bare truth and what was happening in Amritsar had left him dejected and depressed.

It was difficult for him to stay in Amritsar. He met a granthi in the Golden Temple who was heading for Manikaran. He also decided to travel to Manali and live the rest of his life at Manikaran Gurudwara. When he reached Manali, it was winter, and the entire Manikaran area was covered in snow. He had been walking from Kullu towards Manikaran nonstop. He had been hungry and down with fever while walking on the snow. On reaching Manikaran, he fell down, exhausted, and was rendered unconscious.

Later, when he regained consciousness, he realized that he was in an ashram with a saint who had rescued him from imminent death. He had gotten frostbite. He was lying in a room, beside some burning logs, which were giving him a lot of comfort. The saint was relieved that Ram had regained consciousness. He asked him politely, 'Son, who are you and what are you doing in this wilderness? You almost lost your life while lying on the melting ice. I brought you here and covered you with a blanket and was able to save your life.'

'Sir,' he replied, 'I am Ram Singh and I belong to Amritsar. I am looking for solace in these mountains. I want to understand my purpose in life, which has been meaningless after the Britishers killed my family.' He told the saint his entire story of having masqueraded as the Black Panther, who was declared a terrorist by the Britishers and was sent to the Cellular Jail in the Andaman Island.

The saint was impressed by the story he narrated. He said,

'Son, everybody in this world has taken birth for a purpose. I, on my part, can imbibe in you the power to walk on the surface of the Vyas River in front of us. It will take some time, but another option for you would be to become a *karamyogi*. A person who devotes his life to others. Now it is up to you to decide, what course of action you would like to take, whether you would want to achieve the mythical and magical powers of walking on the river or become a karamyogi.

Ram Singh replied, 'Sir, I am disappointed with my life. All my efforts have yielded no results. The cruel British are still ruling the country and are still traumatizing my fellow countrymen.' He took a deep breath and then said, 'One person who could have made a difference is no longer alive. One person who could change have changed the course of history, Subhash Chandra Bose, died in Taiwan last year in a plane crash. Gandhi and Nehru are following the path of non-violence, but that is not yielding the desired results. Non-violent protest is useless and, till now, has borne no results. Did the British make us slaves by following the non-violent path? What rubbish!'

The saint smiled and said, 'Who said that Subhash Chandra Bose died in that accident in Taiwan. Two months ago, he was here, living in the same room that has been allotted to you. His name at present is Gumnami Baba. He left after staying here for some time to reach Germany via Afghanistan and Siberia. His family lives there. I gave him my blessings. Subhash never died in the plane crash; it was a rumour spread by the cunning British, to dismantle the India National Army.'

'Oh,' replied Ram Singh, 'I wanted to join the INA myself

but had no inkling as to how to reach them. No wonder there was a big rumour, as someone had met this Gumnami Baba in Amritsar too. I came to know that Adolf Hitler in the past five years had wreaked havoc in the other European countries. And along with his allies, Italy's Benito Mussolini, and Japan, had crushed the might of the British Empire.'

'Remember son,' he quipped, 'life is like a bicycle. To ride you must balance it. It is also like a boxing match where the referee will not declare you defeated till you refuse to get up. So do not quit. Continue to play the role god has assigned to you.' Ram Singh, with renewed vigour and vitality, got down to serving people. He rowed boats, relentlessly taking the pilgrims and Ashramites across the river.

He went as far as Kutch in Gujarat to help with the digging of wells for people in search of water. In the deserted areas of Kutch, water was scarce. Ram played a stellar role in digging wells alongside other *kar sevak*s and brought relief to hundreds of men and women in Kutch. He spent a lot of time in Gujarat and lived in harsh conditions but worked sincerely for the poverty-stricken people. He did whatever the holy saint asked him to do.

World War II had ceased, resulting in the suicide of Adolf Hitler on 30 April 1945 and the deaths of almost six crore people all over the world. The British Empire had crumbled, and the freedom movement had at last gathered momentum. The British had handed over some part of the government to the Congress Party. The saint who had saved Ram Kumar's life, died in 1947. Ram Singh, alias Ram Kumar, realized that the sacred saint Swani Ram Kumar Kripalu ji had a massive following in ashrams at Manikaran, Dwarka, Pune and Vrindavan. Upon hearing his story, the holy saint was impressed with his deeds as the anonymous Panther and in fighting the British. To the saint, Ram Singh also admitted to having killed several British officers, including the dreaded Thomas Rose and Smith.

The Holy Saint gave him the name 'Revolutionary Guru' and allowed him to live in the ashram and act as a karamyogi.

Days and months passed, and the Revolutionary Guru became an important functionary at Manikaran Ashram, and was also sent to Pune and Dwarka Ashram to manage affairs. People had eulogized him earlier for being the Black Panther, and now he was being revered for being the saint he had become.

On 15 August 1947, he was part of the huge gathering that had assembled at the Red Fort to witness the unfurling of the Indian flag from its ramparts. It was a dream come true for millions of Indians who had suffered almost as slaves under the British. At last, they had achieved freedom.

Years passed, and in 1960 the holy saint Kripaluji met with a brain stroke. He was walking in his garden at 4 a.m. in the morning, amidst the chanting of *bhajans*, as was his routine, when he suddenly fell and died.

It was his last wish that whenever he died, his last rites should be performed at Vrindavan. The one known as Revolutionary Guru, now aged forty-eight years, had been handling Manikaran Ashram all by himself as the managing trustee. He took the lifeless body of his guru to Vrindavan and that was his first ever visit to Vrindavan Ashram.

Almost fifteen thousand people had gathered at the ghats of Yamuna to pay their last respects to the holy saint Swami Ram Kripalu. It was incumbent upon him to enquire about the well-being of his inmates and followers of the cult. He made enquiries about a lady who had met with a paralytic stroke. To his utter shock, he was told that her name was Madhumati. She had been staying at Bardoi and had been living in the ashram as a widow for the past four years.

He made further enquiries and was informed that she had been married to Vikas Chander of Bardoi, a place close to Kashi and famous for manufacturing carpets. Vikas Chander had established a manufactory unit at Bardoi. The couple had no children, but Vikas considered his younger brother to be his only son. Vikas had become wealthy, and when he was forty-five years old, he had been kidnapped by Maan Singh, who had asked for ten lakhs as the ransom amount. When his demand could not be met, he had killed Vikas in a cold-blooded manner.

Ram Singh went to the ashram and was further saddened to know that Madhumati had met with a paralytic stroke and was in a wheelchair. Ram Singh volunteered to help and it was in this way that he met her in person after a gap of twenty-one long years.

At first, Madhu was not able to recognize him. But when he dramatically revealed that he was none other than Ram Kumar, the erstwhile Black Panther of Amritsar, tears rolled down Madhu's cheeks, and a smile seemed to return on her face. He proposed to her, showing his willingness to marry her even if she was suffering from a paralytic stroke.

Ram Singh, alias Ram Kumar, married Madhumati in 1961. Both of them were in their late forties. He took Madhu to the Ashram at Manikaran. After working on her ailment relentlessly and with Ayurvedic medicine provided by the ashramites, Madhu started walking, albeit with a stick.

The Revolutionary Guru also played a stellar role in downsizing the fraudulent spiritual and religious leaders in Vrindavan and Mathura who used dirty tricks to swindle the innocent, religious people. He started publishing a magazine which, using the magicians Gogia Pasha and Surjit Sakar's magic tricks, exposed the tricks behind the so-called miracles of such fraudsters. Gradually, the number of such cults reduced markedly, and the following at Kripalu Dham also grew considerably under his aegis and guidance.

Happy days had finally returned in their lives, and both of them went to Amritsar. He revealed his true identity to the government joint secretary, who allowed him to open his house and mutated the same in his favour. It was in a dilapidated condition. He renovated it and converted it into an ashram for elderly people who had nowhere to go.

He had come a long way from being seven years old when he had seen his brother die at the hands of Col. Dyer or when his entire family had been massacred on his wedding day. Much time had also passed since he had been tortured at Kala Pani and remained marooned on an unknown island. Now he had become the leader of the Hare Rama Hare Krishna cult and was ably supported by his beloved wife Madhu. The Revolutionary Guru would help the destitute and poor people till his last breath.

ARAB STALLIONS

The tiny village was known as Lehra Mohabbat. Situated seventeen kilometres ahead of the bustling city of Bhatinda in the Punjab province of British-ruled India, it was famous for two things: a deep canal that ran alongside the village, from which it got the name Lehra, and second, and more importantly, the legendary love and togetherness amongst the villagers, from which it got the name Mohabbat. Lehra Mohabbat—a village known for love. In the native language, '*lehra*' meant 'stream', and '*mohabbat*' meant 'love'. A stream of love flowed in the tiny town amongst its inhabitants, irrespective of their caste, colour, creed or status.

In June 1909, 670 men, women and children belonging to the Sikh and Hindu communities stood together brandishing swords, *kirpan*s, and any other weapon they could find, determined to protect each other. Some of them had rifles too. And above all, they had their honour. They also knew that before long, a fifteen-thousand-strong British army, a force many times their number, was expected to attack them.

The British rulers of India were angry. They were still seething from the mutiny of 1857 and the nerve of the Indians who had dared to revolt against them. They had suppressed the 1857 Mutiny and arrested the Mughal Emperor, Bahadur Shah Zafar. They had killed the Queen of Jhansi, Tantia Tope, Mangal Pandey, and thousands of other Indians who had of their own accord dared to declare independence. The instructions from England were clear: 'Do not let the grass grow under your feet, finish any mutiny or rebellion before it spirals and has a cascading effect. This is India.'

All the inhabitants of Lehra Mohabbat had gathered together, holding their homely weapons. They were just a few in number, 670 people in total, from the camp to the British Army. But they stood tall in their history. They had grown up, generation after generation, hearing the stories of their ancestors' valour and sacrifice. Now, it was time for them to show courage as their ancestors had shown in the past.

The story of the valour, courage and honour of the inhabitants of Lehra Mohabbat began roughly three hundred years ago. The village was established by Bhai Sant Singh Sambi and had a total population of only 260 people. In 1609, when it was established, it was called Monga. In the next hundred years, its population grew to 580 people; by 1709, it was a village where all the residents lived peacefully. The town was unique, and nothing could shake the bond of love between the people. Not even the cruel, dastardly Mughal rulers.

Way back in 1709, the village had been brutally attacked by Badshah Khan, the powerful subedar of the Mughal army, who brought a force of ten thousand soldiers to bear down upon the village. The 580 villagers stood in unity. Not even a single person from seventy-two-year-old Santokh Singh

Sambi (descendant of Bhai Sant Singh Sambha and head of the village) to young Manjeet Kaur, who was only eleven years old, attempted to flee. The Mughals vastly outnumbered them, but they fought valiantly, sacrificing their own lives to save the lives of the other villagers. Of the 582, 572 were massacred, and some committed suicide to avoid torture. The entire village of Monga showed so much unity and love that the people of Punjab changed its name to Lehra Mohabbat.

Slowly, the village regenerated itself, and now exactly two hundred years later, after Badshah Khan's brutal attack, history was repeating itself. This time, a small but brave contingent of 670 people, led by Sardar Harmeet Singh Sambi, who had also descended from the founder's family, was waiting for an attack. This time, the enemy were not the Mughals but the British.

Harmeet Singh looked at the small force gathered around him, which included his three sons, aged twenty-four, twenty-one, and nineteen. All of them were ready to sacrifice their lives for the village's honour; his wife, along with the other womenfolk of the village, was also ready. Their task was to keep handing out bullets, muskets, swords, and arrows to the soldiers defending their village.

As they waited for the British force to arrive, Harmeet thought about the story his grandfather had told him time and again about the battle of 16 June 1709, when Badshah Khan had wiped out almost the entire village. The attack was instigated due to a very petty issue, which did not warrant the death of so many women, children and elders of the village. It began with the sale of two Arab stallions.

That summer in 1709, Arab traders from Samarkand had

come to Bhatinda to auction two stallions in the open market. Two villagers, Bir Singh and Raghubir Seth, had gone to the market to sell their grain. They had had a rich harvest, and with the money they made from the sale, they bought the two stallions for three hundred rupees each. Excited with their purchase, the two proud owners of the stallions were eager to show them to their fellow villagers of Monga.

They were not aware that Badshah Khan, the subedar of Mughal Emperor Shah Alam II's army, had set his heart on acquiring the stallions and had sent his soldiers to the auction site. The soldiers reached the auction a little late. By then, the stallions had already been sold to the two villagers, Bir Singh and Raghubir Seth. Badshah Khan was furious when he found out that he had lost to two villagers. He was not the kind of man to let go of anything he wanted. He was virtually the commander of the entire north district, from Ludhiana to Ganganagar. Monga village fell directly under his rule. 'How dare anybody take something I wanted?' he lambasted his juniors. His arrogance was at its zenith.

Badshah Khan dispatched his emissaries to the main *sarai* to look for Bir Singh and Raghubir Seth. Finding the two men, his emissaries offered four hundred rupees each for the two horses. In those days, a profit of a hundred rupees was huge, and for a moment, the two were tempted to sell the stallions. But then, they recalled the atrocities committed by Badshah Khan against Sikhs and Hindus and decided not to oblige him. The emissaries knew that failure meant at least fifty lashes from Badshah Khan's *daroga* (police officer). They raised the price to five hundred rupees each. Bir Singh and Raghubir were bemused at how desperate Badshah Khan's emissaries were. They refused to oblige point-blank, knowing fully that Badshah Khan would take the rejection of his offer as an insult to the Mughal rulers.

On hearing that his offer had been rejected, Badshah Khan was livid. He decided to punish them. Bir Singh and Raghubir Seth were picked up, put behind bars and entirely fabricated charges of sedition were slapped against them. Their two stallions were confiscated, and eyeing the property of the Mughal Empire was declared to be sedition. This cognizable offence carried a sentence of at least a year behind bars.

Badshah Khan had ordered the kotwal of the district, Mir Qasim, to frame charges of sedition against them, after which, they were produced before the *qazi* (magistrate), who sentenced them to a hundred lashes, a fine of four thousand rupees and six months' imprisonment. In case of non-payment of the fine, the prison term was to be extended by another six months. Neither Bir nor Raghubir was given a chance to speak. Instead, at the behest of Badshah Khan, they were beaten mercilessly for showing resentment against the might of the Mughals.

News of Badshah Khan's unjust and vengeful actions spread like wildfire throughout the district. People were outraged at the way two innocent people had been treated. But there was little they could do against the all-powerful Subedar, who had the support of Shah Alam II behind him. The emperor believed that anyone who did not follow Islam was an infidel and deserved to be punished. The era of tolerance practised by the Mughal emperor Akbar had gone, and a violent fanaticism had set in by the time Aurangzeb had come to power. Emperor Shah Alam II continued the legacy of hate against Hindus and Sikhs who refused to convert to Islam or who opposed the Mughals in any way. Badshah Khan knew that any action he took against the *kafir*s would have the emperor's blessings. He could get away with anything under the sun so long as it involved targeting or terrorising Hindus and Sikhs.

When the news of the arrest reached the tiny village of Monga, all the inhabitants got together and held a meeting. The youngsters were furious at the way their brethren had been treated and wanted to teach the Mughals a lesson. However, the elders in the village calmed them down and instead asked every villager to contribute towards the fine imposed on Bir Singh and Raghubir Seth so that their sentence would not be extended. They knew that the punishment was unwarranted and harsh, but decided in favour of a peaceful resolution. The foremost thing was to accumulate the exorbitant penalty of four thousand rupees imposed by the qazi at the behest of Subedar Badshah Khan.

Within minutes, the women of the village came forward with their gold ornaments and handed over the money towards the fine. Others sold and contributed whatever they could. They deposited this in the court of the qazi at Bhatinda and, with folded hands, requested him not to extend the sentence of Bir Singh and Raghubir Seth.

Mir Qasim, the kotwal, was a good man and had merely been forced to fabricate charges against the two prisoners on Badshah Khan's direct orders. Unlike the subedar, he respected the law and knew that the two men had been illegally detained. But he was powerless against the continued atrocities committed by the Mughals. Everyone knew that

Badshah Khan had a penchant for cruelty, but no one had expected him to stoop so low as to imprison innocent people who had purchased two Arab stallions in an open auction. Neither were they thieves nor anti-establishment. The sedition charges levied against them were completely false.

On his part, Mir Qasim treated the two prisoners well. His respectful attitude and belief in the equality of all human beings went a long way toward soothing Bir Singh and Raghubir Seth's frayed tempers and any desire for revenge that they might have harboured.

After four months, the two detainees were released on good behaviour on Mir Qasim's recommendation to the qazi. And after an hour's walk through the muddy roads of Bhatinda, they reached their village amidst much fanfare and cheering. No one had expected them to return before their sentence of six months.

Even though he was glad to have his father back, Bir Singh's son, Balbir Singh, could not forget how unjustly the Mughal subedar had thrown his father in prison for a crime he had not committed. His young blood recoiled at the memory; every cell in his body thirsted for revenge. He would wake up at night plotting ways to make Badshah Khan regret what he had done. Other inhabitants of the village were also humiliated and angry at the insult, but slowly, the village elders had calmed them down. Over time, the inhabitants of the village swallowed the insult and moved on with their lives.

But fate hadn't yet played its entire hand. Not long after this incident, Badshah Khan's son got married and decided to give his friends, who had come from a far-off place, a good time. He instructed the kotwal to abduct young girls from a nearby village to entertain his friends through the night, after which they would be let off. The Mughal rulers would often send the kotwal to pick up young girls who were molested and later sent back. No case of complaint was registered, and the girls had to bear the brunt of the harrowing incidents.

Mir Qasim was appalled at the suggestion and advised that it would be simpler to hire nautch girls. But the imperious and high-handed son of Badshah Khan insisted and said, 'No, I want to give my friends the pleasure of seeing young girls perform some folk dances at my wedding and who better than the daughters of kafirs and infidels!' He suggested picking up girls from the nearby villages. It was also one of the ways to teach a lesson to them for the impudence they had shown by refusing to let go of the stallions.

Mir Qasim was upset by this strange demand and expected Badshah Khan to talk sense to his son and put an end to it. But Badshah Khan was even more intoxicated than his son. Instead of reprimanding him, he shouted at the kotwal to immediately follow the orders and instruct the village to present ten girls from Monga before him at the Diwan-e-Khas. They would be sent to the haveli where his son's friends were lodged. Noticing Mir Qasim's hesitation, he dismissed him and summoned one of his senior army commanders to get the job done.

Badshah Khan agreed with his son. He indeed had the perfect village in mind, Monga. The inhabitants had not raised much of an objection when he had unjustly taken the two Arab stallions and thrown the two owners of the horses into prison. Where better to request permission to be absent than from the shrewd Badshah Khan? The girls of the villages would certainly dance and perform during festivals such as Deepawali, Baisakhi, Teej, etc., but would certainly not dance in front of Badshah Khan's guest. He told his army commander to go to the village and inform them of his instruction, and to explain to them that this was not a request but a command.

The army commander had heard stories about similar demands made in the past by Mughal emperors, but never had the subedar of a district done so. He tried to caution the subedar that if such an incident were to go out of hand, it could reach the ears of the emperor and arouse his anger. The villagers of Monga were unlikely to take such an insult quietly and were sure to put up a resistance. But Badshah Khan was in no mood to listen. He was drunk on power as he was the subedar of the entire district. He thought he could do anything he wanted.

After leaving the subedar's haveli, the army commander met the kotwal, who told him that it would be wiser not to obey the master's orders, since he was not in his senses. Instead, he had already arranged for nautch girls, disguised as simple village girls, to reach Zumzum Haveli, where the bridegroom's friends were staying. This way, neither Khan nor his son's friends would ever get to know the truth. A potential crisis could thus be averted. The arrangements they made went as planned. Mir Qasim and Badshah Khan had properly briefed the nautch girls, and his son's friends believed they were indeed young girls from Monga village who had come to perform folk dance. What Mir Qasim had not anticipated was the fact that Badshah Khan's son had, on some occasion, visited the nautch girls in the bazar to witness their dance. He recognized two of them and created a furore over this issue.

The outcome of their meeting was that they would send twenty dancers, ten males and ten females, who would perform in the open courtyard. Mir Qasim agreed to the proposal and somehow convinced Badshah Khan to change the venue and agreed to arranging such a performance.

The next day, around thirty-two villagers reached Bhatinda with musical instruments to perform at his son's wedding. After the *nikah* (Islamic term for marriage) culminated, he complained to his father about the trick that had been played upon him by Mir Qasim, and the commander flew into a rage and ordered both his commander and kotwal to bring the girls from Monga or face supervision and fifty lashes each.

When news reached Monga, the villagers were shocked. Yet again, they were being insulted and shown their place. This was too much. Youngsters from the village rose in anger. They wanted to send a *jatha* (armed parade) to Bhatinda to publicly clarify that nothing of the sort would ever happen. Again, the elders intervened and calmed those down, saying it was just a rumour and that the goodwill of the village had been built over many years, and it would be unwise to tarnish it. But Mir Qasim came with twenty soldiers and confirmed that such instructions had indeed been given. He had somehow tried to salvage some decency by mentioning that Badshah Khan was impressed by the folk dances performed by the villages on festive occasions, and he wanted the same performance at his son's wedding which was scheduled for the next day.

Young Balbir Singh could not take Badshah Khan's cruel treatment towards his father and the villagers. He was not ready to let this go so easily. He summoned three of his close friends to the canal, and they discussed the atrocities of Badshah Khan, which had crossed all limits.

All four youngsters were incensed. Enough was enough. Balbir said that their spiritual tradition taught them to practise love and tolerance and not to attack others first, but it also taught them not to keep quiet in the face of continued injustice. They were not cowards. It was one thing to accept defeat, but totally another to let someone keep tyrannizing them. The subedar had dismissed the residents of Monga village as weaklings who could be pushed around at will. They had not dared to object when he fabricated charges against them or when he confiscated their stallions. Next, he would show off that he could pick up their sisters and then he would restrict them from using the canal for irrigation purposes. It was time to teach him a lesson. Badshah Khan had mistaken their decency for weakness. Balbir Singh coaxed his friends to rise to the occasion and show the wicked, scheming subedar their strength.

The four friends came up with a plan. They decided to be discreet and not include any of the village elders in their plans lest they try and talk them out of it. They decided not to tell Bir Singh or Raghubir Seth either, though they had suffered the subedar's cruelty directly. The time for sitting passively and allowing the subedar to continue tyrannizing them was over.

A month later, their chance came. One night, the moon was completely hidden behind the fog. The foursome quietly left the village, hiding swords, knives and kirpans under their shawls, and made the long walk to Bhatinda. Due to dense fog, it took longer than anticipated to reach Bhatinda, but once there, they stealthily made their way towards Badshah Khan's palatial haveli. As they crossed the stables, they could see two stallions standing inside an enclosure. They were the same stallions that had been confiscated from their elders.

The youngsters quickly saddled the two horses, and just as they were about to take them out of the stables, the guard who had been dozing suddenly woke up and raised an alarm. He moved forward to stop them, simultaneously calling for help. One of the youngsters, Sant Singh, took out his knife and stabbed the guard. Alerted by the commotion, other guards rushed forth. The four youngsters had no intention of getting caught. In the skirmish, two other guards were also stabbed to death by the Sikhs. It was the wee hours of the morning, and it was bitterly cold. Nobody got to know about the killings unleashed by the four young men from Monga. By the time the bodies were discovered, the two stallions were gone, and no one knew who had taken them away or where.

Badshah Khan, with three of his guards dead and two precious stallions stolen, did not take long to figure out what must have happened. He was furious and sent off his spies to Monga to procure information about the stolen stallions.

His spies came back a few days later with their report. Three youngsters from Monga, led by Bir Singh's son, were behind the killing of the guards and the theft of the stallions. They also informed their subedar that most of the villagers did not endorse their actions, and many heated arguments reprimanding them had ensued. Only Bir Singh and Raghubir Seth had seemed pleased by Balbir's daring feat.

Nevertheless, the news spread like wildfire in all the nearby villages and towns. Jalandhar, Ludhiana, Amritsar and Ganganagar; everywhere, people spoke with admiration about the youngsters from Monga who had the guts to reclaim the stallions that belonged to them. Badshah Khan became a laughing stock. Soon, people from nearby villages began bringing gifts to Monga, praising the youngsters for their courage. Only the elders of Monga were silent. They knew that the Mughal subedar was not the kind to get insulted and stay quiet. They knew that he would take his revenge and try to punish the offenders.

And sure enough, smarting from the insult, Badshah Khan went to the court of Shah Alam II and told him that Monga was full of infidel Sikhs and Hindus, who disrespected the Mughals. The Mughal honour needed to be restored, and these kafirs needed to be taught a lesson. Shah Alam II was a weak ruler who spent much of his time intoxicated in his harem. It was easy enough for the subedar to convince him that if this disrespect was not repelled, it could lead to a full-fledged revolt. To clinch the argument, Badshah Khan told the emperor that he had bought two thoroughbred Arab stallions as a gift for none other than Shah Alam. Not only had these stallions been stolen, but three guards had also been killed by the kafirs, the youngsters of Monga. That was it; Shah Alam became furious. He commanded Badshah Khan not only to capture the youngsters but also to hang them publicly.

And so, riding at the head of an army of soldiers belonging to the emperor, Badshah Khan set out to take his revenge. He first took three thousand soldiers, including a hundred cavalrymen, to the village of Monga and sent an emissary to the state that if the four youngsters surrendered, the rest of the villagers would be spared. Otherwise, they would meet the same fate as the guards at the stable: death. The killing of government officials was a punishable offence. Besides, the stallions would have to be returned to Badshah Khan, or the wrath of the mighty Mughal army would descend on the village.

With that demand, Badshah Khan had crossed a line. The elders of Monga, who had always tried to find peaceful solutions, decided that enough was enough. They would fight for their honour to the last man, even if they were outnumbered. Subedar Khan had taken things too far. Moreover, the vengeance seeker was sure to make more unbearable demands if they conceded this time. The time had come to show Subedar Khan that this village would not tolerate suppression any longer. They would rather fight it out than succumb to his unreasonable demands.

And thus ensued a battle between the 580 villagers of the village of Monga and the mighty Mughal army, a battle that began with the unlawful seizure of two Arab stallions by Subedar Khan. The entire village assembled in the central courtyard near the Gurudwara, where swords, knives and kirpans were distributed. A group led by a man named Ram Kumar was assigned to guard the left flank of the village and prevent entry from that side. Some of the elders, like Raghubir Seth and Bir Singh, were asked to defend the rear portion of the village, where an attack was unlikely due to a narrow lane, which made entry on horseback almost impossible. The women were asked to move onto the roofs of their homes and throw stones and boiling oil on the Mughals.

The remaining villagers, a contingent of about two hundred fifty people led by Balbir Singh, waited in the main courtyard to face the Mughal army. Khan's army was cocky and overconfident. They had thousands of soldiers, while the villagers were only a handful. Moreover, they had superior weapons and army training, while the villagers had no battle experience whatsoever.

The Mughals thought that within a few hours, perhaps sooner, the battle would be over. All the villagers would be massacred, and they would be able to go home for dinner. But Badshah Khan's army was in for a surprise. They had underestimated the simple inhabitants of Monga. They had never seen people so determined to fight for their honour. They had no idea how much strength there was in those rebels.

The first attack by Subedar Khan's army was repelled with such ferocity by the villagers that the central column of a thousand Mughal soldiers was stunned, and many ran back to save their lives. From an elevated hill, Khan watched Hindus and Sikhs slashing away at his army with full force. Many villagers died, and many were grievously injured, but they fought on as if driven by a higher purpose. As if they had a long overdue score to settle.

After suffering huge losses in the first attack, Subedar Badshah Khan returned the next day with a stronger contingent of another thousand men. These men also met the same fate. Many were killed, and others ran back to save their lives. Khan had not realized how narrow the lanes for entering the village were. Only four horses and a few foot soldiers could enter at a time to attack. The moment they entered, the villagers pounced on them with so much force that they had to run backwards. Several ambushes were carried out, and several strategies were adopted over the next few days, but the villagers' determination was such that the assaults were repulsed with heavy losses for the Mughals. Badshah Khan realized that against such determined defendants, his three thousand soldiers would not be sufficient.

Here was a village where young and old, Hindu and Sikh, fought valiantly together while his soldiers kept retreating to save their lives. He needed a better plan to finish off the villagers. He ordered his troops to retreat to Bhatinda, where they would strategize on an alternative route to descend upon the village at the same time. A loud cheer went up as the villagers saw the mighty Mughals retreat like cowards, and that too, against the inexperienced, ill-equipped villagers. Last rites were performed for the dead, and some Mughals bearing white flags were allowed to take the dead bodies of their soldiers.

However, the villagers knew that their victory would be short-lived. Subedar Khan was not the kind to tolerate defeat. He was like an injured tiger that would not rest till he had demolished the entire village. They used the time to get ready for the next attack. The womenfolk took charge of the rations, preparing large grains in the Gurudwara storeroom. Many people from the nearby village donated whatever they had, cash, jewellery and other possessions, to them, which helped them to buy new weapons. Two villagers, Lakshman Seth and Buta Singh, were sent in disguise to Bhatinda to try and gather information on Khan's next move.

They came back with the news that while locals in Bhatinda, Ganganagar, and nearby villages were rejoicing at Monga's victory over the Mughals, Emperor Shah Alam II was furious with Khan for bringing disrepute to his name by letting a tiny village army of a few hundred people defeat the great Mughal army. There were rumours that Monga's, courage had inspired uprisings in other areas such as Jhajjar, Jattan, Jamalpur, Meerut, where *jagirdar*s had begun to rebel and raise their heads against the Mughals.

Emperor Shah Alam II could not allow that to happen. He immediately ordered reinforcements from the garrisons at Jalandhar and Lahore to be sent to the aid of Subedar Khan. The emperor took direct charge of battle strategy. Instructions were given to Khan to demolish the villagers' houses to create space for the entry of a large army the launching of a full-fledged attack. Moreover, the village was to be attacked from all sides, irrespective of human losses, and the army was to use all the force at its disposal against the villagers. Humiliated by his earlier defeat, the arrogant Khan had been forced to listen obediently to the emperor's orders. He had fought many battles in his lifetime, but this was the most humiliating defeat he had ever suffered. The emperor ordered him to assemble a large contingent of fifteen thousand soldiers, including eight hundred horse riders, and thirty long-barrelled cannons were sent. There were to be no mistakes this time.

After preparations were complete, Subedar Khan marched once again to Monga village, his son riding by his side. The villagers were waiting. They had set up barricades to prevent the Mughals from destroying their houses and widening the lanes into the central square. They had laid stones and rocks on all four entrances to the village. They knew they were vastly outnumbered, but they stood together, to the last man, woman and child. They would fight with courage, and if death came, that would be God's will.

The Mughal army, led by Subedar Khan, moved forward, sweeping aside all obstacles in its path. Houses were ruthlessly destroyed to make space for the cavalry. After a pitched battle, Khan's soldiers entered the village from the rear side, killing all the villagers standing guard there. Though cornered, the villagers faced the onslaught like true warriors. Balbir Singh and Buta Singh charged frantically at Khan's son with such vigour that he was killed. Balbir Singh was badly injured, but he was satisfied. He had vindicated the village's pride by killing the cruel Badshah Khan's son, who had tyrannized them so frequently. The women who had congregated on the large terrace of the Gurudwara continuously threw stones and boiling oil on the Mughals. They knew what would happen if they were caught alive. When they saw the Mughals breaking open the steel gates of the gurudwara, they jumped into the well, and one by one, all perished. The battle had been ferocious, and Badshah Khan, unable to bear the loss of his son, met with a heart attack when he saw his body.

On the Mughal side, the casualties were 301 soldiers. On the Monga side, 572 villagers gave up their lives in the battle, the youngest only eleven years old. The remaining eight had been sent away earlier with the two Arab stallions to an unknown village in the hills. By the end of the battle, not a single person was left in Monga village.

The Mughal army searched everywhere for the horses. Many people in neighbouring villages were questioned and tortured to give information. All the houses, shops and religious places were searched, but no one in the Mughal army could find the two Arab stallions.

In his memoirs, written some years later, Emperor Shah Alam II was honest enough to praise the villagers who had given one of the toughest fights to the Mughals. He emphasized that while the Sikhs and Hindus had bravely died defending their honour, Subedar Khan had lost his life only due to his arrogance and inflated ego.

Stories of Monga's courage spread across Punjab; the village was renamed Lehra Mohabbat as a tribute to the Hindu and Sikh inhabitants who had stood united and died while defending their honour. Many songs were composed in praise of the valour of Lehra Mohabbat.

Several years later, in 1711, one of the eight survivors returned to the village and, with the help of influential relatives, reclaimed his land. After seeking permission from the new Subedar Mir Qasim, he rebuilt the demolished houses in the village one by one. Mir Qasim had always been sympathetic to the villagers who had been brutally killed on a non-existent, irrelevant and trivial issue.

With his support, the village began to revive. The land belonging to their ancestors was again cultivated, and, following many good harvests, the town gradually prospered. The new generations that followed all grew up on stories about the sacrifices made by their ancestors, the inhabitants of the village which had once been known as Monga.

And now, in 1909, over two hundred years after the attack by the Mughals, history was repeating itself. Once again, a small contingent from Lehra Mohabbat faced an army many times its size. This time, the army belonged to the British, who ruled over India and considered Indians an inferior race which would have to be kept in its place. In some respects, the British were crueller than the Mughals who had treated the locals as their subjects. The British treated them as slaves. The British believed in the adage 'divide and rule'.

Again, the incident began without the villagers' fault. A few days prior, four inebriated British soldiers had misbehaved with Harmeet Singh's wife. They had been drinking heavily by the side of the canal, when Harmeet Singh's wife, along with a friend, came to get some water from the canal. The British soldiers spotted the two women and began to make lewd remarks. Then one got down from his jeep and blocked the path of Harmeet Singh's wife's. He tried to caress her. With great difficulty, she wriggled out of his grasp and ran towards the village. Her friend was frozen with terror and unable to move. The four British soldiers grabbed her and raped her, one after the other, laughing at their easy conquest. The woman kept crying for help, but no one came to her aid as no one was able to hear her cries.

By this time, Harmeet's wife had reached home. Harmeet was furious when he heard what had happened and rushed blindly towards the canal with his close friend, Manmohan. The four Englishmen were still drinking and boasting about their lust-filled afternoon. They had not expected anyone to show up. Harmeet and Manmohan caught them by surprise and stabbed them with their swords. It was all over in a matter of minutes. They then picked up the dead bodies of the four Englishmen, tied them to the jeep and pushed the jeep into the deep end of the canal. It sank within minutes. There was no trace left of either the vehicle or the four British soldiers. Harmeet and Manmohan had put them to death without a minute's thought about the ensuing consequences.

Sir Johnston Murray, resident commissioner of Ganganagar district, sent police to investigate the disappearance of the four British soldiers. They had last been seen at the canal near Lehra Mohabbat, after which they had not returned. The police officials made enquiries, but no one at Lehra Mohabbat gave them any information about the killings, even though everyone knew exactly what had happened.

A few weeks later, about a kilometre downstream, near Rasouli village, a few children were swimming in the canal. When one of them dived a little deeper, he saw four bodies tied up in a jeep. An alarm was raised, and the jeep, with its water-bloated bodies, was pulled out by the police. Experts were summoned. In the next three days, a post-mortem was conducted, and an autopsy report was presented to the resident commissioner along with evidence and probable cause of death.

The resident commissioner took this episode very seriously. Four Englishmen had been killed; the culprits had to be found and punished. Consequently, fifty policemen swooped down on Rasouli village and questioned every resident. However, the investigations did not reveal anything since the villagers of Rasouli genuinely had no idea about the murders. Many youngsters were tortured, but nothing concrete came out.

The resident commissioner called expert divers to understand the river course better. Within a short time, the divers were able to correctly ascertain that the jeep had been pushed into the water near Lehra Mohabbat, where the four British soldiers had last been seen. Lehra Mohabbat was mainly occupied by prosperous Sikh farmers, a community that the resident commissioner especially despised for their ferocity against what they called British injustice. His own grandfather's father had been killed in a battle led by Maharaja Ranjit Singh, the ruler of Punjab, in 1839. He had heard enough stories of the nerve and audacity of the tenth Sikh guru, Guru Gobind Singh, and of the formidable force of the Khalsa. This was not a community that was easily scared. It was indeed very likely that the residents from this very village had killed the four British officers. They would not be allowed to get away with it.

He took permission from the Governor-General, Lord Hastings, to show the Sikhs that no matter what the provocation, even if the British soldiers were drunk or at fault, they were not to lay a finger on an Englishman. They needed to be punished, and an example needed to be set before the natives to showcase the might of the British and to reinforce the fact that they were the rulers. He believed that every British death should be avenged by killing at least fifty natives. Lord Hastings, who equally despised the natives, issued an order for the arrest and public beheading of the accused who had dared to kill four English soldiers.

A superintendent of police conducted a thorough investigation to identify the criminals. He came back with a report accusing the entire village of conspiracy to kill the four soldiers. Lord Hastings refused to believe that a whole village could be responsible for the deaths. At best, this could be the handiwork of a few people. He warned the inhabitants of Lehra Mohabbat to come clean and reveal the names of the culprits, else the entire village would be held responsible and razed to the ground.

Again, there was a situation almost identical to the one that had occurred two hundred years ago when Subedar Khan had threatened the entire village. The village had united and fought to the death, then. Now, once again, the bond of love brought all the inhabitants of Lehra Mohabbat together. It was a bond based on their proud history, and it had to be seen to be believed. Each person was willing to die rather than hand over their brethren to the British. No one whispered a word against Harmit Singh or Manmohan.

By then, the British had come to know that the four officers had raped a woman and had been killed in revenge. As always, the British had different rules for themselves and for the natives. No matter what offence the British officers may have committed, it was the natives they wanted to see hang.

The residents of Lehra Mohabbat stood against them in a wall of solidarity. Once again, they faced an army. Once again, they had only simple knives and swords, while the British army had far superior weapons, including cannons. Once again, the honour of the village was at stake. Each person knew that they were unlikely to win against the British, but no matter; they would give them the fight of their lives. And, this time too, the enemy would underestimate the strength and determination of the villagers of Lehra Mohabbat.

Harmit Singh, along with his three sons and other villagers, waited. The drumbeat sounded louder by the minute as the far superior British army marched closer. Harmit Singh had instructed the villagers not to fire or attack the enemy until they entered the main foyer of the village near the Gurudwara, which, over the years, had been rebuilt into a haveli-shaped structure with nine-inch-thick walls.

The British, too, had heard the stories of how the ancestors of these villagers had not cowered before the tyrant Subedar Khan, and had fought bravely against the Mughal soldiers, killing three thousand and one hundred of them. The British officer-in-command was cautious in making a move, even though he knew his force vastly outnumbered the 720 inhabitants of the village. The British soldiers felt demoralized at this slow approach, while the villagers used the time to gain momentum.

It was noon when the British fired the first volley of bullets and cannonballs. It was rebuffed with full force by the villagers. The British began to unleash cannonballs, one after the other, which brought the village walls crumbling down. Their shelter gone, the villagers were soon exposed. They came rushing together into the foyer where the British had foolishly assembled. Forty Sikh horsemen came from the narrow lanes, brandishing swords, and attacked the British with such force that the British soldiers dropped their weapons and ran for cover. Sir Johnston Murray, watching this sudden attack by a handful of Sikhs, decided to retaliate by leading an attack with eight hundred selected horse-riders in his army. He came rushing to the spot and encircled the small contingent of Sikhs and Hindus fighting tooth and nail against the British soldiers. Once again, the villagers' determination was such that many British soldiers ran to save their lives.

Sir Murray was able to disarm the Sikh horse riders, only to see, much to his surprise, village women climbing onto the roof of the Gurudwara and pelting stones and throwing bucketfuls of hot oil onto the soldiers. Another contingent of fifty villagers emerged from the left side of the Gurudwara, taking the British soldiers by surprise. The battle raged, and it seemed that the 720 villagers would defeat the demoralized British force. But they were completely outnumbered, and one by one, they began succumbing to the bullets of the British soldiers.

The battle raged for three hours, and when the women and children looking down from the terrace of the Gurudwara saw their husbands and brothers being killed, they ran down with sticks and knives to continue the battle, which they knew they would eventually lose.

Sir Johnston Murray's chief commander waited for his orders. There were now mostly women and children left, but Sir Murray showed no mercy. He looked at his commander and turned his thumb downward. The signal was given, and in no time all the women and children had been slaughtered. The 720 villagers of Lehra Mohabbat had all been put to death. To make sure no one survived, they were shot multiple times.

As Sir Johnston saw the bodies of the dead villagers sprawled all over, he paused in amazement. If other natives of this country showed the same kind of unity and courage, British rule would come to an end sooner than anyone could possibly imagine. He could not fathom what had motivated the entire village to unite and lay down their lives for one another. He shook his head; he thought they were made to do what they had done. He ordered that villagers from other villages be brought and funerals be performed as per Hindu/Sikh customs. Before turning away towards Bhatinda, he bowed before the dead bodies and heaved a sigh of relief that he had put an end to the brave warriors of Punjab.

Little did he know that not far away, in the Ropar district, a child named Bhagat Singh had already been born, who would give British rule a jolt that would shake its foundations and pave the way for India's freedom.